AFTER
THE
weekend
LOVE AND CARE

SILVIA VIOLET

Silvia Violet

After the Weekend by Silvia Violet

CHAPTER ONE

_____

AVERY

I set the grocery bags down on the counter. "Sean, did you get the vodka?"

Sean leaned out from the bathroom, buck naked.

"Felicity will be here any minute. She doesn't want to see your naked ass."

He waved me off. "She's not interested in any of this."

"That doesn't mean she wants it waving in her face. Hell, I don't want it waving in my face either."

"Ha. You should be so lucky."

I flipped him off. "Vodka?"

"Of course I got the fucking vodka. Gin too."

"Good." I had a feeling there would be a lot of drinking tonight. I hadn't seen Felicity since she'd returned from her honeymoon, and I was nervous as fuck. She'd said she was fine with me dating her new father-in-law. (If something that stripped me raw and made me long for Graham like he was part of me could be called dating.) But now that Felicity was back to reality, would she feel the same way? My feelings hadn't changed at all, but why would anyone not want a man like Graham who exuded the perfect combination of sweet and hot-as-fuck?

I'd Skyped with Graham several times since the weekend of the wedding, and we'd texted every day—many, many times every day. He still seemed as… obsessed? enthralled? desperate? as I was, and he was coming back in three days. I couldn't wait. I'd jerked off at least twice a day remembering everything we'd done and fantasizing about what was still to come, like maybe fisting? Yikes! But also, oh God, that's hot.

I unloaded my grocery bags as quickly as I could. I'd gotten what I needed to put together a charcuterie and cheese board, and Felicity was bringing a dessert of some sort. I really hoped it was her mom's lemon cake, but I figured it would more likely be something she picked up on her way here.

I glanced at the clock. Shit. Fifteen minutes. I hoped she'd be late. I'd missed her like crazy, but I wasn't sure I was ready to see her yet. Or ever. She was no doubt going to ask questions I didn't want to answer, and Sean would just make it worse. He had no filter. Maybe I should send him away.

"Sean?"

He stepped out of his room wearing nothing but tiny briefs.

"What the fuck? You've had plenty of time to get dressed."

"I was busy."

"You're supposed to be helping me set up."

"I know, but somebody sent me this link and—"

"Tell me you were not jerking off right after you showered."

He shrugged.

"Dear God, Sean. Get yourself together. You're twenty-five, not fifteen."

"A man is never too old for self-pleasure."

"Maybe if you're that horny you should just go out tonight." Sean used to go trolling clubs every weekend, but lately he'd been more likely to lie on the couch, complaining about not having a man, than out there, hooking up.

"No fucking way am I missing the Felicity reunion, not when you fucked her new father-in-law at the wedding."

"Remind me why we're friends."

He blew me a kiss. "Because you love me."

"Go get dressed, and stop making it sound like I jumped him during the ceremony."

He cackled as he shut the door to his room. I no longer cared if I got the cheese and meat unwrapped before Felicity arrived. I needed alcohol. I found the vodka in the freezer, poured a healthy amount into a glass, added a little cranberry juice and gulped some down, making myself cough. I should've come home earlier, so I would've had time for several of these before confronting Felicity. I really needed to be buzzed to deal with this night.

But before I'd even finished my first drink, Felicity knocked on the door. "Dammit, she's never early except when I don't want her to be."

Sean snorted. He'd finally dressed and was now placing olives in a dish, though at the rate he was eating them, there wouldn't be many left for me and Felicity.

"Of course she's early. She's dying to find out what's up with you and Daddy."

"Ugh. Stop calling him that."

"Never."

I gave him my best death glare. "Sean, I'm seriously warning you."

"Fine. I'll behave… Maybe."

"Sean."

"I'm sorry. But you have to admit—"

"Yes, I know it's hilarious, because he's Carter's dad and—"

The doorbell rang again. "For fuck's sake, let me in. I'm melting out here."

"No need to make sure it's her," Sean said, smirking at me.

I opened the door, and as soon as I saw Felicity, I realized how very much I'd missed her. I pulled her to me, and we hugged until she pushed me back into the apartment. "I've got to get out of this heat."

We were having a record-breaking June, and it was miserable out there. "Come on in," I said as I took a bag from her.

"I got those petit fours you love from Sugar Fetish. Mama says she'll make you a lemon cake if you come to dinner on Sunday."

"Dinner?" Dawn's lemon cake was the best thing ever, but I wasn't sure it was worth being interrogated over dinner.

Felicity rolled her eyes. "You know, a meal in the evening. You sit down and eat food."

"But Graham will be here."

"Mama wants you to bring him."

I sighed. "And I suppose you and Carter will be there."

She nodded seriously, playing her part well. If I hadn't known her like I did, I might not have noticed how hard she was trying not to smile.

"We are so not ready for this."

"Yes, you are. Carter and I are fine with you guys being together, so there's no reason for it to be a problem."

"No reason. Felicity, do you hear yourself?"

She frowned, but I could tell she was still acting. "Are you ashamed to be with someone his age?"

"What? No."

"So…"

"Felicity, you cannot be serious."

She cracked up then. "The look on your face."

"You know this is fucking awkward."

"Yeah, for all of us, but you know how Mom is. She wants to get to know him better."

I also knew that Dawn thought Graham was way hot. "Is she trying to encroach on my territory?"

Felicity laughed. "Of course not. I thought he was all about cock anyway."

I grinned. "He really is."

"Ok. That's… no."

"Trust me," Sean said. "He's seriously into cock and ass and all kinds of kinky shit."

Felicity put her hands over her ears. "La, la, la."

"We'll stop. Or at least I will." I tugged on one of her arms. "No more sex talk, but I did kinda need to talk about what the fuck I'm doing."

"Falling for a man in forty-eight hours?"

I wanted to deny it, but she was absolutely right.

"Damn right he did," Sean said. "And he's been pining for him ever since. God, the pining. You're so lucky you've missed it."

I glared at Sean. "Will you kindly shut the fuck up?"

Sean stuck his tongue out as he grabbed yet another olive from the platter. "Are we going to eat this stuff, or is it just supposed to look pretty?"

I rolled my eyes. "Come on."

Felicity followed me to the bar. I poured her a drink, and we stood around the counter eating right from the platter and cutting board. Felicity told us all about the honeymoon, insisting we must all go to Trinidad one day.

Then, because I was still nervous talking about Graham, I let Sean tell all about his angst with his current job and how he might go back to school for something else, but he wasn't sure what.

Felicity seemed as unenthusiastic about this idea as I was. "Sean, you hate being in school, and you changed majors like three times."

He huffed. "I don't see why I should have to keep doing something I hate, just because I used to think I'd like it."

"How about a different job in your field?" she asked. "There are lots of different types of jobs for technical writers."

"Ugh. It's all so boring."

I didn't know what he thought it was going to be like, but I kept silent.

"Enough of your indecision," Felicity said. "I want to know what the fuck is going on with Avery."

"Well, last night I caught him—"

"Sean! Don't you dare," I screeched.

Felicity rolled her eyes. "Out with it, Avery. You're in love with him, but you've known him less than two weeks, so you're freaking out. What else?"

"Damn it. How do you do that?"

"I'm sure I didn't cover it all."

I sighed. "Yeah, you kinda did."

"Come on." She made a circling motion with her hand. "Out with it."

I glanced at Sean, and he nodded, having heard my silent plea. "There's not quite enough drinking going on here for me. I'm going to head out."

"Thanks," I mouthed. Sean often pretended to be an asshole, but he's actually a totally decent guy. He knew I needed time alone with Felicity.

He hugged Felicity and then me, whispering "be honest" before pulling away. Sometimes I forgot how clearly he saw me.

"Talk," Felicity said as soon as he was gone.

"I'm scared. I... This is too fast and too much, and I've fallen so hard when I never meant to."

She nodded, studying me for a moment before saying, "I think this could be really good for you."

"Or I could get badly hurt."

She shook her head. "Don't push him away because you're scared. I see you considering it, but you won't know how this goes unless you try."

"I don't have the nerve to anyway. Just thinking about not seeing him again hurts."

"Wow. Tell me I was never this bad with Carter."

"You were determined rather than desperate. That's just who you are."

"True." Felicity took a sip of her second gin and tonic. "I always knew when you found someone it would be intense like this. You're so passionate about what you love."

"How can I love him already?"

"Because he fits you."

11

I poured more vodka into my glass. "And you somehow knew that he would."

"No. I knew you'd think he was hot as hell and want him to fuck you. I didn't know he was The One."

"Why do you think he is now?"

"I see it. On your face and his."

"Really?" I knew I was in over my head, and I was sure Graham cared about me as more than a casual fuck, but I didn't think…

"When Carter and I had lunch with him, and I guessed he was the one you'd spent the night with, he was so happy when he talked about you, and so concerned that you would be angry. Every time Carter texts with him, he mentions you."

"What? Seriously?"

She nodded.

"Graham and I talk every day. I thought maybe this—whatever it is—would fade, maybe he'd change his mind about coming back, but he hasn't, not yet anyway."

She laid a hand over mine. "Enjoy it, Avery. Don't hold yourself back; let him see the real you."

He does. "I think he did from the start."

"Then maybe he really is The One."

"So you don't think I'm crazy?"

"No. I think you might be really lucky, almost as lucky as I am."

"I honestly thought you would tell me to back off, to not rush into this. You're always cautious."

"I'm cautious, but you're not. As fabulous as I am, I don't want you to be me."

I pulled her to me. "I love you."

She hugged me tight. "I love you too. Now tell me all about what you have planned for this weekend."

I proceeded to do just that. Well, not *all* I had planned. There were things, lots of things, that might traumatize her. Or they might not, and she would torture Carter by telling him. She did have a cruel streak, even if she was my best friend.

CHAPTER TWO

GRAHAM

Leo pulled a bottle of Macallan 12 from his desk drawer and poured us each a glass. I'd been busy all week trying to catch up on work after taking time away for Carter's wedding. I'd worked most of the past weekend, but that was fine, because it meant I could take this weekend off to have more time with my boy.

Leo leaned back in his seat, propped his feet on his desk, and studied me for several moments. "Whoever he is, he's good for you."

I took a swallow of scotch. Avery was good for me, but I was hesitant to tell Leo about him, which was unusual. Since I'd met Leo shortly after my divorce, he'd been my confessor for whatever was good or bad in my life. He'd seen me at my worst and truly wanted what was best for me. But I'd been avoiding him since I got back to Charlotte. Part of me was worried I might jinx this fragile thing between me and Avery. Despite talking to Avery every day and knowing how perfectly we fit, the longer I was away from him, the more I imagined he thought his time with me was just a hot diversion, not… love. Of course I only dared say that word to myself.

"What's wrong?" Leo asked.

"Just me being stupid."

He glared at me, using an expression that would have a sub on his knees immediately.

I exhaled. "So I met someone at the wedding."

"I was right, then."

"Aren't you always, but this is big. It's… Fuck, I'm scared of it."

"Wow. I've never seen you this rattled over a man."

"He's… I don't know. It's like I saw him, and I knew he was special, and then after…"

"You fucked?"

I laughed. It wasn't like I had any reason to be shy around Leo. We'd fucked each other, and we'd done scenes together. He'd taught me a lot of what I knew about how to discipline a sub without hurting them more than I meant to. But Avery was different from any man I'd been with before.

Leo laid a hand over mine. "Are you sure you're all right?'

"Yes, I'm better than I've ever been, actually."

"I feel like there's a 'but' coming."

I sighed. "The man who's making me happy, he's Felicity's best friend, her Twink of Honor."

"Holy shit. I mean, I know you like twinks, but…"

"Carter knows. He says he's ok with it."

"So this wasn't a one-time thing?"

I shook my head. "I'm going back up there on Friday. We've talked every day. I know it's too much too fast, but I can't help myself."

"Whoa. What exactly are you feeling for this guy?"

"A lot. Maybe… God, Leo, I think I'm in love."

His feet hit the floor, and he leaned forward, putting his elbows on his desk. "No fucking way."

"I know it's crazy."

"You've known him what, a week? You spent two days together."

I tossed back the last of my drink. "Three, but I knew the first night."

"Graham, are you sure about this?" he asked as he poured more scotch for each of us.

"You said he was good for me."

"You look good. You sound happier and more relaxed than you have in ages, but maybe—"

I sighed. "I knew you'd think I should slow down."

"I'm not trying to judge you or what you feel, but I don't want you to get hurt."

I tried to think of a way to help Leo understand the instant connection I'd felt with Avery. "You want to know the first thing he said to me?"

"What?"

"Oh, Daddy."

Leo choked on his drink.

"I didn't think he really meant it like that, but I could see his need to submit, to have someone else take control."

"Oh, fuck."

"I told myself I shouldn't start something, not at Carter's wedding, especially not with Felicity's friend. But he sought me out and asked for exactly what I wanted most."

Leo swirled his drink around, seeming to consider his words. "So it's like that with you? Daddy and boy?"

I nodded. "And it's so good, better than I ever thought it could be. I can't imagine finding someone more compatible sexually."

"Damn, no wonder you look good."

I grinned. "Yeah, I'm very… satisfied."

He rolled his eyes as he took a sip of scotch. "And you really think this could be more than just sex?"

"I know it could. I don't want to push too hard, but waiting two weeks to see him again has felt like a lifetime."

"Damn, that's… I can't even imagine." He looked away for a moment as he rubbed his thumb along the side of his glass. "There was a time when I thought maybe… But no. Things haven't worked out."

"Oh, God. Do you mean us? Did you think we could be more for each other?"

He shook his head. "I wished we could, but I knew better."

I took his hand and squeezed it. "I wished it too. You mean a lot to me, as much as anyone in my life."

Leo smiled. "I know we're meant to be friends, to be…"

"Family?"

He drank the last of his second scotch. "Yes. Definitely not lovers, not in any serious way."

"I can't be what you need."

"A man who longs to take the pain I want to give?"

I nodded.

Leo sighed. "I know. And I didn't mean you just now, though that is a regret. I just meant that I used to believe I would find a man I was compatible with, but I'm so tired of doing scenes where I don't feel anything. It's all become so mechanical for me, and lately it's just too hard to go through all that negotiation with someone who only wants to get off. It's been ages since I've so much as spanked someone unless I was doing training or a demo."

I could hear the pain in his words, and I hated it. "You'll find someone. Don't give up."

"I shouldn't be complaining. I have what most men dream of. If I wanted, I could have a line of twinks down the hall, waiting their turn with me."

"Leo, you deserve to be loved and cared for. It's okay to want that."

He shrugged. "What I have is pretty damn good: a business of my own, friends I can count on, men to be with whenever I want them."

If he didn't want them, though, that hardly mattered. I could feel how uncomfortable he was, letting himself be this vulnerable, so I decided not to push.

Leo toyed with his empty glass for a few moments, then said, "I guess now that you've found a boy, you don't want to go look for someone we can play with out there." He gestured in the direction of the public part of the club.

I frowned. "I thought you said you didn't—"

"I know. I just thought maybe if we looked together…"

"Leo—"

He shook his head. "I'm in a weird mood, that's all. Maybe it's because Carter is married now. The idea that your son has found his happily-ever-after, and we're… Well, *I'm* without any prospects for that."

"I'm probably crazy to think Avery wants this to be a long-term thing."

"Why wouldn't he want you?" Leo asked. "You're incredible."

"Tell that to my ex."

Leo wrinkled his nose like he'd smelled something offensive. "How bad was it, seeing her again at the wedding?"

"As ugly as I expected, but Avery knew how to make me forget all about it."

Leo smiled. "He sounds perfect. When do I get to meet him?"

"You want to?"

"If you think he's The One for you, then it's my duty to vet him before things go much further."

I laughed. "Not this weekend. It's only our second time together, but maybe in a week or two."

"Good. I need to go to Asheville anyway."

"Yeah? How come?"

"You know how you keep harping on me to expand my empire?"

I nodded. I'd told Leo several times that Succumb was doing so well he should look into starting another club.

"There's a club in Asheville that the owners want to sell. I thought I'd take a look."

I tried not to be offended that he hadn't mentioned this before now. "When were you planning to tell me?"

"I was debating if I really wanted to consider it. I didn't want to say anything until I was sure."

"You do."

He frowned. "But running Succumb takes so much time."

"Because you don't delegate."

He snorted. "You're one to talk."

He was more right than I wanted to admit. "Fine. Let's make a pact to turn as many tasks as we can over to someone else."

"You'll have to if you want more time with your boy."

"Yeah. I have a feeling I'll be spending a lot of time in Asheville, and it would be great to have you there too. I've got a condo without a tenant and one where the lease is coming up for renewal in two months. I can give you one of those if you end up buying the club and needing to be in Asheville for a while."

"By 'give' I hope you mean rent, because I'm going to pay you."

I shook my head. "I'm not charging you rent."

Leo gave me his best Dom stare.

"You know that doesn't work on me."

He grinned. "A few times it has."

"Only because I was in the mood for it."

"And tonight you're all Daddy?"

I laughed. "Yeah, I am."

"We'll work out the housing if I decide I want the club."

"And I'll ask Avery what he knows about the place."

Leo poured us each more scotch and lifted his glass. "To future endeavors."

I clinked my glass to his and smiled, thankful to have a friend like him.

***

Later that night, I lay on my side, watching Avery on my laptop. He was seated on the edge of his bed, legs spread, jerking off. And he was close, almost there. I wanted to see his teeth sink into his lower lip, his head fall back, cum shoot from his cock, but what I wanted more was to make him wait, to see him flush as he stuck out his lip when I said, "Stop!"

Avery's hand fell to his side, his chest rising and falling, pain evident on his face before he gave me the pout I'd been waiting for. His lips looked so puffy. He'd painted them blue for me tonight, and he was hot as hell like that. His eyes were wide as he stared at me, silently begging. Part of me wanted to give him what he wanted, but I also wanted him desperate when I got there in three days. I wanted to test his obedience. He'd told me he thrived on challenges, so I was going to give him one.

"You're not going to come again until I see you on Friday."

"Wh-what?"

"You are not allowed to touch yourself. I'm going to trust you. Just like you can hold yourself without restraints, I trust you to keep your hands off your cock without me there to monitor you. Only absolutely necessary touches are allowed, nothing else, and no rubbing against the mattress either. Is that clear?"

"Daddy," he whimpered. "Please at least let me come now. I know you like to watch."

"Boy, I gave you an order. Your choices are 'yes, sir' or your safeword."

Avery glanced down.

"Look at me, boy."

He did. I saw concern in his expression. "You can do this. I'm challenging you because I care, because I want you to be proud of yourself."

"Yes, sir."

I smiled then. "Much better."

"It's just… I never go more than a day without jerking off."

"Then you need to learn some discipline. Daddy wants you desperate for it when he gets there."

He groaned. "Fuck. That's so hot."

"Then do this for me."

"Yes, Daddy. I will."

"Good boy. We'll talk and text, but no more Skyping before my visit."

He looked relieved. "Thank you, Daddy. It would be so much harder to hold back if I saw you again."

"I know, boy. Now go get some sleep."

Avery looked down at his swollen cock. "That's not going to be easy."

"You'll have to figure it out, because I need you rested on Friday night."

He groaned. "Daddy, you're killing me."

"Go and be good."

"Goodnight, Daddy."

"Goodnight, boy."

CHAPTER THREE

AVERY

He's going to know. He's going to know. The words
ran through my mind over and over as I packed my bag
to go meet Graham. Ever since he'd told me I wasn't
allowed to come, that was all I could think about. Last
night I'd given in and jerked off. Twice. I was not a
good boy, and now I was sure Graham would know
what I'd done.

"You leaving soon to see your sugar daddy?"
Sean asked.

"Dammit, Sean. It's not like that."

He gave me a pointed look. "He owns so many
condos he just happened to have one free where y'all
can shack up."

I exhaled, trying to suppress the urge to strangle
Sean. "I don't want him for his money. This is… it's a
hell of a lot more than that."

I could tell Sean realized he'd gone too far. "I'm
sorry. I know it's more to you. I was just teasing, but I
do expect you to tell me how swanky his condo is."

"He owns a development company, so of
course he has a lot of rental properties. I don't know
that this one is particularly fancy."

Sean huffed. "It's a condo downtown. I think
they only come in Rich People Approved. You'll be
able to walk to dinner with your man, lush it up, then

stumble home and fuck all night, probably with a view of the city."

I grinned, because he was right. This was going to be an amazing weekend.

"You know I'm totally jealous."

I stared at him. "I thought you didn't want a man of your own."

"A weekend of the fine life with a hot hookup would be perfect, though."

"Go find yourself a sugar daddy. With that ass it shouldn't be too hard."

Sean slapped his butt cheek. "Damn right. I work hard for this. But you know that's not really what I like."

"Older men?"

"Yeah."

"And being told what to do?"

"In bed that can be fine, but in the rest of my life, hell no. I'm a free man."

Sometimes I wondered if Sean protested just a bit too much. I'd seen him with men at our favorite club, men who'd brought him to his knees. He'd liked it a lot until he'd remembered he didn't want to.

It would take me all night and probably more to analyze Sean, and I had a date. I quickly double-checked that I had everything. "All right, I'm out of here. I'll be back on Monday night."

"Unless you convince him to stay longer."

I rolled my eyes. "That's not going to happen."

"Are you so sure about that?"

"He's got work to do, a business in Charlotte, a life in Charlotte." Something I tried not to think about too hard.

"But now he also has you."

I groaned. I wanted him to have me right that minute.

Sean grimaced. "Go before you make any more of those sex sounds."

I flipped him off and slipped out the door, practically running for my car. But once I got in the driver's seat, I remembered how certain I was Graham would figure out that I'd disobeyed. I was sure he'd punish me for it, harder than last time.

I sighed. The spanking he'd given me had been so hot, but it had hurt like hell too, and I was scared there'd be more than a spanking this time. I shivered, unsure if I wanted him to find out or not.

***

Graham pulled the door open, and my breath left me. I'd seen him over Skype several times, but there was something about his presence that couldn't be seen on screen, something that made him even more gorgeous in person.

"Hi," he said.

"Hi."

He stepped back, and I entered the condo. I had no idea what to say. He seemed nervous too, which I hadn't expected.

If he'd just ordered me to my knees or pressed his hand against my cock, that would have been better. When we were Daddy and boy, not just Graham and Avery, everything was easier.

"So, um, did you have a good drive?" I asked, because apparently I'd become my mother.

"It was fine. There was a lot of traffic, but it's a June weekend, so…"

I nodded. "Yeah, tourists."

Having no idea what to say then, I glanced around the condo. It was modern but still inviting. The walls were pale salmon, and the furniture and accents were a mix of gray and cream. The sofa looked solid, like it would hold up if he bent me over it. In front of it lay a plush rug with swirls of cream, gray, and black. The rest of the great room had hardwood floors, but I could see myself kneeling on that rug by the glass coffee table, waiting to see what Daddy would ask of me next.

The kitchen had high-end appliances, which made me wonder if Graham could cook. The thought of him in the kitchen, reading glasses on as he looked over a recipe, apron tied around his waist, was way too hot.

The silence had gone on too long so I said, "This is place is nice."

"Thank you. These condos rent better, even to long-term residents, if they're furnished. So I had a decorator fix it up for me."

"Oh, you didn't pick this out yourself? Because it fits you."

He smiled, like me noticing made him happy. "I gave input, and I do like it. I might go a little warmer if it were for me, though."

"The wall color saves it from feeling cold."

He smiled again. "That's one of the things I chose. Come on. You can put your bag in the bedroom."

I followed him, watching his ass and wanting to find a way to ask him if we could be Daddy and boy for a little while, just until we were used to each other again. But I didn't, because I thought maybe that was the wrong thing to say. I just wished he wouldn't be so polite, so different from the first time we'd talked when I'd met him and he'd simply said, "Do you like what you see?"

We hadn't worried about what we said then, or at least I hadn't. I'd been expecting a hot night, not whatever this was. A future? Something that threatened to break my heart?

The bedroom was a beautiful Caribbean blue. The bed was nowhere near as massive as the one at the Misty Mountain Lodge. It looked like a queen, and we could make do with that.

Who was I kidding? I'd let Graham have me on a cot or the hardwood floor if that's what he wanted.

He cleared his throat. When I turned to look at him, I realized I'd been staring at the bed for a long time.

"I… Um…"

"Put your bag down, boy."

I smiled and hoped he saw the relief on my face. "Yes, Daddy."

I set it by the large upholstered chair that stood in front of the single window. I wanted Graham to fuck me in the chair too.

When I turned back to him, Graham grabbed my shirt and yanked me against him, pressing his lips to mine. I was desperate for him, and he seemed ready to eat me alive. By the time he pulled back, I was panting like I'd run downtown instead of driving.

"I missed you," I said.

"I missed you too, boy. Have you been good?" He looked me up and down. Then he palmed my cock, squeezing it hard enough to make me jerk.

"Daddy," I whined.

"I asked you a question, boy."

I couldn't lie to him, and I was sure he knew that. "I touched myself, Daddy. I made myself come."

"How many times?"

Say once. He won't know. "Two times. Both last night. I'm so sorry, Daddy."

"Strip and lay over the end of the bed." His voice was stern, and I shivered.

"Daddy, I—"

"Boy, you've misbehaved and now you need to be punished. Trust me to deal with you as I see fit."

"I… I do, Daddy."

"Then do as you're told, or I'll add to your punishment."

I scrambled to obey.

When I was naked and displayed for him, he squeezed my ass, pulling my cheeks apart. "When I'm done I'm going to fuck you so hard and deep. It's going to be amazing."

"Please."

He laughed, the sound harsh. "You've got a long time to wait, boy. I brought rope. May I tie your wrists?"

"Yes, Daddy." The words were out before I even thought about them. I wondered if there was anything I wouldn't let him do.

He tapped my ankle with his foot. "Open wider."

I widened my legs, and he teased a finger over my hole. "So hot. I'd love to see you with a spreader bar holding you open."

"Oh my God, please."

"You're so eager to serve." He chuckled, and the sound seemed to vibrate over me. "I don't have one with me, but I'll remember how much that turns you on."

"You remember everything, Daddy. I want to make you happy."

"You do, boy. I'm so glad I found you."

"Daddy," I whimpered.

He ran a hand down my spine. "Shhh. I know what you need."

I didn't know how, but he did. I needed him to punish me. Maybe last night when I'd jerked off frantically, enjoying being defiant, I'd known I'd need this. But I also knew that if he asked me not to touch myself again, I would obey. I would hold off no matter how long he kept me from coming or how badly my cock ached.

He stepped away and returned with a length of bright blue rope, the same color as the lipstick he'd asked me to wear the last time we'd Skyped. "Bring your wrists together and cross them."

When I did, he wrapped the rope around them, securing them together. I hadn't realized colored rope would be so erotic, but I loved the way it stood out against my skin.

Graham smiled at me. "You like that, don't you, boy?"

"Yes, Daddy."

"I knew it would look amazing on you."

"You know just what I need."

"That's right, boy, and now you need my belt on your ass, so you'll remember when I tell you to do something. If you don't trust and obey me, then I can't give what you need. To help you learn, I'm giving you pain before I pleasure you."

"Yes, Daddy. Please."

"You want to hurt for me?"

"Yes, Daddy. I need to give you that."

"Oh, my boy." He stroked my cheek. "I know you want to be good. I'm going to give you five strokes with my belt, and then we'll take a break. After that, I'll give you five more, but I'll hit you harder. You're to keep your cock away from the mattress. I don't want you getting any friction. You will not come until I'm inside you, but you can make any sounds you want: cry, scream, beg."

"Yes, Daddy."

"If you need me to stop, what do you say?"

"Red." My heart was pounding and the sheet under me was already damp with sweat. "Daddy?"

"Yes, boy?"

"I'm scared."

"Shhh." He rubbed my back. "I know what you can take."

Before I could respond, he cracked the belt across my ass, and I cried out, squirming to get away.

He took hold of my hips and yanked me back from the edge of the bed. "Stay put. I know you can."

Another slap.

"Fuck! Fuck, that hurts!"

Another one.

I writhed, kicking my legs. "Please, Daddy. I'm so sorry."

"That's good, boy, but I'm not going to stop."
Crack!

Tears burned my eyes. "Daddy, please. Please!"

"Take it, boy."
Crack!

Tears spilled over until I was sobbing. "It hurts so much more than your hand."

"I know, boy." He dug his fingers into my ass and pulled me open. I cried out, but then I felt his warm breath against my hole.

"Daddy?" The word came out strangled as he licked a line from my balls to the base of my spine. I pushed back against his mouth, too desperate to worry if he was going to punish me for being so needy.

He tongued me, pushing at my hole, then giving teasing flicks. I groaned, tears drying on my face as I worked my hips. I held myself back from the mattress, though, knowing I had to obey Daddy, no matter how much I wanted to rub my cock on the bed. My ass throbbed with bright pain, but it seemed to make me come alive, to become nothing but sensation. Graham rimmed me, driving his tongue deeper, dribbling spit down my crack, making me mindless with desire.

"Daddy! Daddy. Need. Want."

He pulled back, and I cried out, "No!"

"Yes, boy. It's time for the belt again."

"Please, Daddy."

"I know what you need, boy."

"Daddy, I know, but—"

He caressed my back. "Do you trust me?"

"I want to. I really want to."

"Good. This is going to hurt."

What did he think the other strokes had done? If this was worse, I wasn't sure I could take it.

"What's your safeword?"

"R-red."

"And if you use it?"

"You'll stop."

"Will I be angry?"

"N-no."

"Will I think you're not a good boy?"

"No." I said the word with more confidence this time. He wouldn't demand more than I could handle, and that allowed me to relax into the mattress.

"Take a deep breath, and let it out."

I did. He brought the belt down on the exhale. Pain bloomed over me, and I couldn't get another breath.

He hit me again.

"Daddy!"

"Boy, do you need me to stop?"

"Can't breathe. Hurts so much. Please."

"Three more. Can you take them for me? I'll go fast."

I was crying again. "Please don't stop. I need this." I hadn't planned to say those words, but I realized they were true.

Pain exploded across my ass as the blows came so fast I couldn't separate them.

Then Daddy was on the bed with me, brushing away my tears, kissing my cheek and my forehead.

"So good. I'm so proud of you. You thought you couldn't take it, but you did, and you were so beautiful as you struggled."

"Daddy, please. I hurt so much but I'm so hard. I need to come. Please." I wasn't even sure if I'd managed to speak actual words or just nonsense. My head was buzzing, and the room had gone fuzzy at the edges.

"Yes, boy. You've been so good. You deserve to come."

"Please!" I worked my hips like I was trying to fuck the air.

Daddy brushed a hand over my hair and then stood.

I tried to keep still, but when he worked a lubed finger into me, I pushed back hard, taking it deeper.

He slapped my ass, making me gasp.

"I'm in control, boy."

"I don't need prep, Daddy. Just fuck me."

"I'm going to prep you, because I have no intention of going slow once my dick's in you."

I wanted to argue, but Daddy wouldn't like that.

He caressed my sore ass as he worked a few fingers into me. "Good. So good, boy."

He finger-fucked me until I thought I would die. Then finally his cock was there, pushing into me, stretching my sore ass and making me burn inside and out.

"You ready to be fucked, boy?"

I couldn't decide which I felt more, pain or pleasure, as he thrust into me again and again, holding my hips still, so I couldn't get any friction.

"You can come now, boy. You don't have to wait anymore."

I tried to reach for my cock, having forgotten I was restrained. I struggled against the bonds. "Daddy, I need… I can't…"

"You can. You don't need to touch your cock. You just need me inside you, filling you, owning you, taking this ass that's mine to spank, mine to fuck." He slammed into me as he gripped my abused ass. "Feel how it stings, boy, how you ache. But you're going to be good now. You're going to come for me without being touched."

Holy shit. I started to believe I could. I was so close. "Yes, Daddy. I want to come for you."

He tilted my hips, the angle making him peg my prostate. I was right at the edge, so ready to go off. "More. Fuck me, Daddy. Fuck me harder."

He did, slamming his hips against my stinging ass.

"Yes. God, yes! I…" I lost the ability to speak as the world lit up like a flash had gone off in my face. Heat, pain, and pleasure mingled until I didn't know which was which or whether the world even existed anymore. I thought I screamed, but I wasn't sure sound actually came out.

Cum shot from my cock, and Daddy slowed his strokes. "Yes, boy. Squeeze my cock with that hot little ass. Give me all of it."

"Fuck, oh fuck."

When I was done, I sagged against the bed. Daddy pulled out, and I whimpered. "So sore."

"I know. I'm going to help you with that, but first I want to see you covered in my cum. I want to mark you, because you're mine."

His words made my cock jerk, trying to revive itself. "Yours, Daddy. Make me yours."

I felt cum spatter my back as he shouted my name. Avery, my real name. The real me, not just a role. He wanted all of me.

"Cover me in cum, Daddy. I want to be messy for you."

He growled as he finished. I was wet and sticky and certain I could feel every stripe of the belt on my ass. But I'd never felt better.

Graham stood and laid a hand on my back. "I used you hard, boy, but now I'm going to soothe that sore ass and clean you up. Let's get you on the bed on your side."

I lifted my knee onto the mattress and groaned. My legs were stiff from standing while he belted and then fucked me.

"Easy, boy. Just scoot up far enough to lie down." I did, and he walked around the bed. "Here." He lifted my head and eased a pillow under it.

"Daddy?"

"Yes, boy?"

"It hurts more now."

"Did I go too far?" He looked so worried I had to reassure him.

"No, I could've stopped you. I chose this."

"I'm going to put some arnica gel on it, that will help, but I want you to be completely honest with me. Even if you chose it in the moment and regret that now, tell me so I know to hold back more next time."

I took a deep breath, letting myself feel the pain instead of trying to push it away. My cock twitched as I settled into the sting of it.

When I opened my eyes, Graham was smiling. He must have seen me smile when it started to feel good again.

"You didn't go too far."

"I'm glad to hear that."

He brought me a warm washcloth and cleaned the cum off me. Then he made me drink a full glass of water before retrieving the gel for my ass.

"Roll over on your stomach. This will help soothe you and make your ass heal more quickly."

I did as he said, but I yelped when he first touched me. Even the gentle brush of his fingers hurt my heated skin, and the salve was wickedly cold.

"I'm so proud of you, boy," he said as he carefully worked the gel into my skin. "I pushed you hard, maybe harder than I should have with something new."

"I trust you, Daddy. I really do." I turned my head to look at him, and when I saw the expression on his face as he stared down at the welts, my breath caught. He was in awe of what he'd done, what I'd taken, what we'd shared. I would do it again just to see that look.

"Thank you, Daddy."

"You're welcome, boy."

I reached for him, and he squeezed my hand. "You did know what I needed."

"Thank you for telling me that. You really are amazing, boy."

"I want to be. I'll be better next time; I promise." And I knew I would be.

He spent a long time rubbing my feet and calves. Then he massaged my shoulders and ran his fingers soothingly through my hair until I was nearly asleep.

"How are you feeling?"

"Mmm. Good." My ass ached, but it was a dull pain now. I would have been content to lie there forever if I hadn't been hungry. Before I could say that, my stomach rumbled.

"You need food."

"I do."

"Hmm." Graham pulled his phone from the pants he'd apparently discarded before fucking me. I didn't even remember him getting undressed. "I had reservations for us at Limones."

"You remembered it was my favorite?" We'd talked about Asheville restaurants the last night we'd spent together when we'd finally gotten too fucked out to do anything but lie there.

"I did. But we were supposed to be there thirty minutes ago, and I didn't respond when they called me."

"Oh." I couldn't really be disappointed. "This was better."

He smiled. "This was necessary."

"If I'd been a good boy, I'd be eating at my favorite restaurant now."

"That's true."

"I'm sorry, Daddy."

He kissed the top of my head. "I know. Since it's the weekend, it won't be easy to get into any of my favorite places without a reservation. If there was food here, I'd cook for you."

"I was wondering if you cooked when I saw the kitchen. It looks like a chef lives here."

"I'm no chef, but I can cook fairly well." Heat rushed to his face. Seeing Graham blush was one of my favorite things in the world. I resolved to make it happen as often as I could, which just might earn me the belt again.

"I hope you will cook for me sometime, but we can go out tonight. It doesn't have to be any place fancy, does it?"

"I wanted to take my boy out, show him off, give him something nice, since he gives me so much."

"Oh, Daddy, thank you. But what if I took you to another favorite place? It's a Korean food truck, and they're always at one of the breweries by the river on Fridays. There's lots of outside seating, and it should have finally cooled off by now. And—"

"That would be lovely. Avery—" I noticed the switch from "boy" to my real name and nodded. "Let's just be us while we're there. I think our discomfort when you first arrived shows that we need more time to get to know each other outside of our role play."

"As long as we can have more of this later."

He slapped my thigh. "Greedy boy. Go get dressed."

CHAPTER FOUR

───────────────────

GRAHAM

Avery walked toward me, carrying a round of beers for us. I hadn't been able to take my eyes off him as he'd ordered at the bar. His ass in the tight red jeans he wore was enough to draw attention from many of the brewery's patrons. Walking had to be painful as the fabric rubbed against his abraded skin. I'd asked him if he wanted to stop by his apartment and find something else to wear, or if he wanted to order something in, but he'd shaken his head, saying he'd earned the punishment. He also wore a black t-shirt and just enough makeup to make him ridiculously beautiful. His lipstick wasn't very obvious, but his lips appeared slightly plumper and redder, like he'd been biting them.

He'd grinned at me when I'd pulled on my sport coat, complete with elbow patches. "Wow. That is such a Daddy outfit."

"You approve?"

"So much it's hard not to kneel."

"I wouldn't say no to that later."

He'd grinned, then he must have remembered how sore he was, because he looked concerned.

"Don't worry, baby. I won't be using your ass tonight. It needs to heal, but there's plenty we can do without me fucking you."

He brightened again. "There certainly is."

Just as he reached the table, the guy at the food truck window called our number.

"I'll get it," Avery said, setting the glasses down.

"No, let me." I started to stand, but Avery put his hand on my shoulder.

"I like doing things for you."

When he brought back our bulgogi rice bowls, he set mine in front of me along with a fork and a napkin. "Do you need anything else? I could get us extra hot sauce or—"

"You don't have to serve me like this, not here."

"Oh, I know. I'm just…"

Then I realized what was going on. "You don't want to sit down, do you?"

His cheeks pinkened adorably. "No."

"Sit down, Avery. Right now."

I kept the words low so other people wouldn't hear the command in my tone. I didn't want to embarrass him, but I wanted him to know that he wasn't going to get away with hovering. I'd offered to stay in, but he'd insisted on this. I knew I was breaking the rules we'd set, but it felt necessary. He couldn't stand up all night.

"Yes, sir." He said the words with a cute little pout, and I thought about how I could torment him for that, but I wasn't supposed to punish him if we weren't in a scene, was I?

"Are you looking for more of what makes you afraid to sit down?" I asked, wanting to be sure I was reading him correctly.

He licked his lips and looked away. "Not really."

I raised my brows, giving him my best "Daddy" look.

"I'm sorry. I… I don't really know, exactly."

"Sit down," I said again, more gently this time.

He did, slowly and carefully. I couldn't help but smile as he bit his lip.

"I didn't think about how hard these chairs are," he said.

I glanced around and saw an open table just inside, one with a cushioned bench. "Come on. Follow me."

"Where are we going?"

"Inside." I grabbed my beer and food, and he did the same. When he saw the new table, he smiled widely. "Thank you."

"You're welcome. I like taking care of you, remember?"

"As much as you like spanking me?" he asked, his voice barely audible.

"More."

"Oh. Wow. That's…" His cheeks were red, and he looked both turned on and shocked. "I didn't expect to like that part so much. It's never been anything but part of a game for me."

I nodded. "Me either. I think it's going to take us a while to figure out exactly what we want and how much and when."

"Yeah, I think so too." His voice was breathless and his eyes wide and full of lust. As much as I wanted to, I wasn't going to drag him out of there and get us off again, not now, anyway.

"Eat. You're going to need plenty of energy later."

He smiled. "I can't wait to see what you think of the food. I hope you like it as much as I do."

I scooped up a bite, making sure I had some beef, some kimchi, and rice on my fork, and it was every bit as good as he said it would be. "This is amazing," I said, too enthusiastic to even wait until I'd finished chewing.

Avery grinned as he finished his first bite. "Isn't it?"

I laid a hand over his. "Thank you for sharing this with me."

"I want to share everything with you." As soon as the words were out, I saw fear in his eyes.

"Don't worry. I want that too."

He frowned. "Why is the sex part so much easier than the talking?"

"Because our bodies know what they want and they don't let our minds get in the way. Now we're overthinking everything, or at least I am."

He sighed. "Yeah, me too."

"Let's just enjoy our night, okay?"

He nodded.

"This beer is awesome too. I meant to give you a fancy evening out, but I think this is even better."

He grinned. "I don't expect you to treat me like a princess, you know."

"But I like doing that." I let my gaze sweep over him, imagining him in heels and a princess dress. Whoa, what was that about? Heat rushed to my cheeks.

Avery was staring at me. "What?"

I shook my head. "Nothing."

"That was not nothing. Tell me."

"I just started thinking…" I could feel the heat creeping up my neck into my face. "Do you ever wear heels or dresses? I know that just because you like makeup, doesn't mean you…"

He squeezed my hand. "I can't tell you how much it means to have you acknowledge that there's not some femme package deal or anything. I only wear things like that occasionally, for an event or a few times for a scene, but I'd wear anything you asked me to."

I had to swallow before I could speak. "Anything? Really?"

"Really. Heels. Rope. A butt plug."

I almost choked on my beer as I remembered using the remote-controlled plug on him the weekend we'd met. "No more sex talk."

He grinned. "Am I disturbing you?"

"You're asking for your ass to be even more sore."

"No. No definitely not."

I started to say something snarky, but then he looked up from his food. "Shit. I forgot."

"What's wrong?"

"Felicity's mom wants us to come to Sunday dinner at her house."

I started to respond, but he kept talking, the words coming so fast I could barely keep up.

"I know we just started this, and I don't expect you to say yes, because it's weird and Carter will be there and Felicity's grandma, and they'll ask all kinds of questions that we don't have answers to, and—"

"Avery!"

He blinked. "Yeah?"

"It's fine. We'll go. I am not in any way ashamed of what we're doing. I know it'll be a little awkward, but I have no intention of ending this any time soon." *Or ever.* "So we're going to have to get used to being around friends and family as a couple." As soon as I finished my proclamation, a wave of insecurity hit me. "Unless you don't… I mean if you…"

"No. I feel the same way. I want this to last, so I guess you're right. It's just…"

"What? Talk to me."

"They all know how short of a time it's been since we met, and I don't want them judging us."

"Have Felicity or Carter or anyone in Felicity's family said something to make you think they will?"

He shook his head. "No, Felicity is all for us being together, though she did balk when Sean tried to give her details."

I nearly choked. "Details?"

"He 'accidentally' overheard some of our Skype conversations."

"You need your own apartment."

He waved me off. "Sean is harmless."

"He needs someone to teach him some discipline."

Avery tilted his head, seeming to consider that for a moment. "You're not wrong. Did you have someone in mind?"

I pondered that. Leo wasn't into bratty subs, and that's what Sean would surely be. Leo liked men who were naturally submissive and willing to endure whatever he asked. I considered a few of the other Doms I knew, but none seemed right for Sean. "I can't think of anyone who isn't already part of a couple."

"A few months ago, he went out with a guy who seemed like he might be a good match. It lasted for a few weeks, a record for Sean, but then he stopped mentioning the guy. All he would say was that it wasn't going to work. Anytime I try to ask about it, he shuts me down. He's dated a lot of assholes, and we often joke about them, but he won't say anything against this guy. He swears the breakup was his own fault."

"Sounds like there's a story there."

He nodded. "Hopefully I'll pry it out of him one night when he's drunk, but that's enough about Sean. I want to know more about your cooking skills."

I shrugged. "I love grilling, which I know is really cliché for a man my age, but I can also make a very good breakfast. I guess I can do anything basic, and a few more special dishes."

He narrowed his eyes. "Why do I think you're just being modest?"

"My food's really not chef quality, but it is good."

"Cook dinner for me tomorrow. Please. I have to work from ten to five, but if we get up early we can go to the farmer's market and see what we find there."

"You'd really like that?"

He nodded. "No one's ever made a meal from scratch just for me. My mom isn't much of a cook. We ate out a lot, and when she did cook it was just about having something there, not about making it special."

"Baby, I want to make everything special for you."

He sank his teeth into his lower lip, giving me a shy look before saying, "Thank you."

***

After dinner and a few more beers, we walked back to my condo. I could tell Avery needed to go to bed soon. He'd had a long day at work and he'd been thoroughly wrung out by me. He was walking stiffly, and I imagined his jeans felt like sandpaper against his

45

tender skin. When I looked over at him, he smiled up, and I pulled him against me, so glad things felt right between us now. I couldn't believe how nervous I'd been when he'd first arrived. Now we were just as in tune with each other as we'd been the weekend of the wedding.

"Would you like to see some of the makeup I've been working on?" Avery asked as we neared the condo.

"You'd share that with me?" I'd gotten the sense when we'd talked about it before that he was shy about discussing his creations.

"Yeah, I know you will understand."

My heart skipped a beat at those words. "I'm… I'm so glad you feel that way."

"I'm actually wearing lipstick I made right now."

I studied his lips as I fished my keys out of my pocket. "Then I already know I like what you make, not that I ever thought I wouldn't."

"You're not just humoring me, are you?" he asked when I'd unlocked the door and we'd stepped inside.

"Never, boy. Go get your makeup, and bring it out here." I gave him a light slap on the ass to send him toward the bedroom.

When he came back, I was seated on the couch. He knelt on the carpet by the table. The position made sense if he was going to lay the makeup out, but it also felt so natural, having him there at my feet. It was where he belonged. He glanced up at me, and color rose in his cheeks. Had he been thinking something similar?

46

"I don't have a lot yet, but these are a few of the eyeshadows and lipsticks I've created. As well as some cream that helps remove them. I'm trying to stick with natural ingredients as much as I can to make them environmentally friendly and good for sensitive skin."

I picked up a few of the little containers and marveled at them, imagining each of them on Avery. He'd look especially gorgeous in the magenta lipstick. I held it up. "Will you wear this for me tomorrow?"

"You like it?"

"I love it. I love all of these. The colors are so rich."

"It stays on really well, too. And yes, I'll wear it for you. Like I told you before, I'll wear anything for you."

I sucked in a breath, needing a moment before I could speak again. Then I said, "You need to keep developing these. You have so much talent."

"I want to. I wish I could afford to spend more time on it, start my own company, work toward getting them in stores, but right now that's just not going to happen."

I wanted to tell him I could make it happen, but I knew better than to just blurt that out. I needed to think about the right way to offer help, a way he might accept, because I was going to see him follow this dream.

"Pack that up. Then I'll get you ready for bed."

"Oh, I thought we were…"

"I'm tired and so are you. Your ass also needs time to heal."

He still looked unsure, but he said, "Yes, Daddy."

I used a finger under his chin to tilt his head back up so he was looking at me. "Is this okay? To role-play now?"

Avery nodded.

"You know you can safeword anytime, for any reason, not just during sex or spankings, right?"

"I know, Daddy."

"Good boy. Now do what I said."

He packed up his makeup and followed me to the bathroom. I turned on the water to let it heat up and began to undress him. He raised his arms so I could pull his t-shirt over his head. I folded it and laid it on the counter.

"I'm going to be as gentle as I can getting these tight pants off."

"They hurt, Daddy."

"I'm sure they do, but I've appreciated the view."

"Thank you."

I unfastened his pants, careful not to touch his cock any more than absolutely necessary as I worked them open.

I pushed them and his barely there briefs over his ass. He tensed, but he didn't complain.

"Step out of them," I said when they'd puddled at his feet.

He did, and I placed them with his shirt. Then I wet a washcloth and carefully cleaned his abraded ass and his cock and balls. I had to fight the urge to jack him off with the soapy cloth, but this was meant to be about caring, not about sex.

"Daddy?" The word came out all husky. "Are you…?"

"I'm cleaning you, boy, and getting you ready for bed."

"Yes, Daddy."

I removed his makeup next, using the wipes and liquid remover he'd brought with him. Finally, I washed his face with his cleanser. "Rinse off in the sink, brush your teeth, and go lie on your stomach on the bed."

"Yes, Daddy."

"Did you bring pajamas?"

"I brought sleep pants and a t-shirt," he said.

"Good. I'll find them."

When he came into the bedroom, I had the clothes laid out on the bed. He lay down like I'd instructed him and I rubbed more arnica into his ass. He flinched when I first touched him, but then he sighed and sank into the mattress. "That's right, boy, just relax and take some deep breaths."

I rubbed all over the area where I'd belted him. Seeing those red stripes had my cock filling, but I wasn't going to act on it. My boy needed rest, no matter how much I wanted to spend all night fucking him. Maybe another day we'd find out just how many times he could make me come in a single night.

"There. That's good. Now turn over and sit up."

He did what I said, looking relaxed and dreamy. "Good boy. I like when you obey quickly like that."

"Thank you, Daddy."

"Lift your arms."

He did, with no hesitation at all. I loved how natural this all felt. I slid his t-shirt down over his chest, caressing his sides as I did. He giggled when I reached his armpits. "Ticklish?"

He shook his head. "I'm not telling you that."

"Really?" I raised my brows.

"Please don't tickle me, Daddy."

"Since you remembered how to ask nicely, I won't. Not tonight, anyway, since your ass is sore. Another day, though. I'll expect you to tell me what I want to know."

"Yes, Daddy."

"Now lay back." He did, biting his lip as he shifted on the bed.

"How bad does it hurt?"

"Enough to make me remember how incredible it was to feel pain but to still want your belt, need it."

"Damn, boy, that's so hot, and it makes me feel really special."

"You're special, Daddy."

My eyes stung with unshed tears as I brushed my hand over his cheek. "You're the best boy a Daddy could have." I kissed him before he could respond with more sweet words that might do in my resolve to get plenty of rest.

He opened to me, drawing my tongue in, but I kept the kiss gentle and pulled back long before I wanted to. I never remembered just how soft his lips were.

Avery sighed. "I want more, Daddy."

"Not now. I need to get you dressed."

"Do you have to?"

"Yes, because if we sleep naked, I might damage that sore ass."

I was glad his pants were soft, worn flannel that would be gentle against his tender skin. "Lift your feet." He did, and I slid the PJs up his legs. "Now your hips." He winced when I slid them over his ass. Once I was finished, I stroked his chest. "Are you okay now?"

"I'm fine, Daddy."

"Good. Now I'm going to tuck you in."

"Aren't you sleeping with me, Daddy?"

"I'll come to bed in just a little while. I need to get myself ready, but I wanted you settled first."

I pulled the covers over him, and he rolled to his side and curled up. "Sleep well, boy."

"Don't be long, Daddy. I want you here with me."

My heart was melting for him. "I'm just going to change into sleep pants and brush my teeth."

By the time I slipped into bed, my boy was sound asleep. I tugged him to me so his head was pillowed on my chest. He sighed but didn't wake. I drifted off with his weight on me and the feel of his soft skin under my hands.

***

The next morning, I woke before Avery. He'd been so good, not begging me or questioning me about having sex last night, so when I felt his morning erection against my leg, I decided he deserved a reward. I slipped down under the covers, pulled down his sleep pants, and took his cock in my mouth. It only took him a few moments to stir. He groaned and pushed deeper into my mouth, but I pulled back. "How does that feel?"

"So good. Don't stop."

"Do you need to straddle me so you don't hurt your ass?" He had to still be incredibly sore.

"No, it's good like this."

"You can thrust into my mouth if you want to. This is about you. Enjoy this any way you want. You've earned it."

"Thank you, Daddy."

I teased his slit before adding, "The only rule is don't hold back any sounds. I want to hear them all."

"Yes—Oh my God!" he cried out as I sucked on his cockhead.

Part of me wanted to tease him to draw this out, but he needed breakfast before work, and I'd said this was about reward, not torment. There'd be plenty of time to toy with him this weekend. I drew the flat of my tongue up his shaft, dragging whimpers from him. Then I swallowed him to the root, and he gripped the sides of my head. "More. Please, Daddy, give me more."

I was relentless, sucking and licking until he was quivering, his balls pulled up tight. I tugged on them as I teased his hole, and he came, thrusting into me so hard, I had to hold his hips down to keep from choking.

"So good. Daddy, it's so good." He kept muttering those words over and over as I licked him clean.

My own cock was so hard I was right on the edge. A few thrusts against the bed, and I would've lost it, but I kept myself still. Once I'd licked up all the cum I'd missed, I rose on my knees and took my cock in my hand.

Avery's eyes widened. "Are you going to come on me?"

"Yes, boy. Roll over. I want to come all over your welted ass."

"Oh fuck, Daddy." His cock jumped, and I wondered if I could keep sucking him and force a second orgasm from him. That was another thought to store away for the future.

"Is this another reward?" Avery asked as he lifted his ass like he was begging for me to come on it.

"Fuck, yes, it is, boy. You've been so good. You get to have my cum all over you." I loved that he thought of it as a reward. He was so fucking perfect.

It took only a few more pulls, and I was coming on top of the red lines I'd made the night before.

Avery glanced over his shoulder. "Wow, that is so hot."

I ran a finger through my cum, rubbing it into one of the welts.

Avery sucked in his breath, but he arched his back, pushing his ass toward me. "More."

I rubbed more of my seed into his skin and then lifted my sticky finger to his mouth for him to suck. The pull of his mouth made me wish we had time for more, but we didn't.

"Enough. I'm going to shower while you make us coffee. Then you'll shower, and I'll run get us some breakfast at Valley Bakery."

He looked ready to protest.

"Was that too much? If you don't want—"

"I do. It's just surprising, because I would've thought I wouldn't like you telling me what to do outside of bed. I can take care of myself. I'm rarely ever late unless I have to take Sean somewhere, because he's never on time to anything."

I shook my head. "Sean really does need a firm hand."

Avery grinned. "So much. But I'm a mess sometimes, just not when it really matters. I've wished for someone to push me, to help me make hard decisions. And having you organize me just feels right."

"I will push you to be the best person you can, and I'll take care of you as much as you want me to. I don't know where that line is for us. I thought I did, but now…"

"Yeah, same."

We looked at each other for a few moments. Then Avery rose from the bed, and pulled up his sleep pants. "I'm going to make your coffee, Daddy."

He emphasized the last word, giving me a smirk, but also telling me role-playing was okay, at least in this moment.

"It better be ready when I'm out of the shower, boy."

"It will. And I'll have it made just like you like it."

"You remember?"

"Of course I do. I want to please my daddy."

I grinned all the way to the shower.

CHAPTER FIVE

AVERY

Saturday evening was amazing. Graham grilled a pork loin and made a salad with goat cheese and blackberries that he insisted even I could duplicate. No matter how simple the food, having him cook for me was as special as I thought it would be. We slept in late on Sunday, and then after eggs and toast, we spent most of the rest of the day in bed talking, fucking, and watching movies. But inevitably, evening came, and we had to go to Dawn's house.

"We could still run away," I said as we stood on her porch. Graham shook his head, so I took a deep breath and knocked.

"I'll get it," I heard Felicity call.

"Shit. Here we go."

Graham leaned in close, his lips almost touching my ear. "It's going to be fine."

Felicity looked us over when she opened the door. "Damn, you two look nice together. Avery, I haven't seen you this happy in years. He is good for you."

"Thank you," Graham said, his voice soft and sure.

He laid a hand on my back and pressed lightly. I knew he was telling me to go inside. So I did.

Dawn practically ran into the entryway, and Carter was right behind her. Throughout the hugs and greetings, her yorkies raced around our feet, threatening to trip us or deafen us with their shrill barks. I'd crouched down to scratch one of the little devil's ears, when she said, "I'm so excited to hear how this happened."

I grimaced, certain I knew what "this" was even before I looked up and saw her gesture between Graham and me. We were so not telling that story, at least not the detailed version; maybe I could just make something up.

"We just hit it off at the wedding," Graham said. "There's not much to tell."

How did he manage to say that so calmly? I would've stuttered and fumbled through some attempt to say anything other than the truth—that I'd propositioned him for kinky sex, because I was into dominant, older men.

Dawn smiled deviously. "I'm sure that's not the whole story, but I'll accept it for now. Come on, let's get out of the foyer. I've got drinks and appetizers out on the back deck, and Felicity and Carter are trying to light the fire pit."

"Mama, I told you we got it going," Felicity huffed. "I finally made Carter listen to me."

Carter glanced my way, and I made a slashing motion across my throat to discourage him from arguing with her.

When we stepped onto the deck, Felicity's grandmother was there, seated on an old-fashioned metal glider sofa.

"Forgive me for not coming to greet you," she said. "Once I get in this thing, I don't get up again easily. Besides, somebody ought to watch this fire. Those youngins just ran off and left it."

"Granny, it's all contained in the fire pit," Felicity protested.

"You should never leave a fire unattended." Granny shook her head. "This is what comes of you quitting girl scouts."

Dawn looked at Graham, since the rest of us knew this story. "The leader told her she couldn't add fringe and sequins to her uniform, and she never went back."

"Clearly she needed a place that allowed for more self-expression," Graham said, but I could see how hard he was trying not to laugh.

"Mother," Dawn said, "You remember Graham, Carter's father, right?"

"I'm not senile. I saw the man two weeks ago at Felicity's wedding, and it would be hard to forget a man who looks like that." Granny looked him up and down and grinned.

I smirked at Graham, who obviously had no idea how to respond. Finally taking pity on him, I sat down next to Granny to divert her attention. "So, tell me how you've been."

"Oh, I've been fine. Not doing much but fighting bugs and rabbits in the garden."

We rocked gently as the others made small plates of hors d'oeuvres. Graham seemed content with me taking some time to chat with Granny while he talked to Carter. My mother's mother died when I was a baby, and my father's mother was as cold as the arctic sea, so I'd been thrilled when I met Granny. She'd treated me like her own grandchild ever since.

She leaned over and whispered, "You look amazing."

"You like this look?" I gestured to my eye makeup. It was a wonder it wasn't smeared all over my face, since Graham teased me while I put it on, stroking my cock, brushing his finger over my hole, generally working me into a frenzy, and then telling me we'd play more after dinner. The bastard.

She narrowed her eyes, studying me. "I do like that shade of eyeshadow on you, but I meant that you look happy, rested, like you've found your place in the world."

I glanced up to see if Graham had heard her, but he was talking to Carter about a hike Carter and Felicity had done on their honeymoon.

"I… I really like him, Granny."

"I can tell you do. And why wouldn't you?"

"You don't think it matters that he's older?"

"Pish, what difference does that make if you're happy?" She said it like it was so obvious. Maybe it was.

"I am happy. He's everything I've been looking for."

She laid her hand over mine. "Then hold onto him, dear."

"Listen up, everyone," Dawn called.

"Oh boy," Granny said. "It's her turn to be bossy."

"Did she get it from her father?" Granny wasn't afraid to speak her mind, but she didn't have the managing tendencies of her daughter and granddaughter.

"She sure did," Granny said. "But I knew how to put that man in his place when he got like that.

Dawn married an asshole who couldn't appreciate her, but I think Felicity's got it right."

I smiled, glancing over at Carter and Felicity. His arm was around her as she poked at the fire, which she hadn't left alone for more than a minute. "I think she did. "

"And if you marry Graham, we'll all be one crazy interconnected family."

My pulse sped up until I felt breathless. Marry Graham? "Graham and I aren't... I mean we haven't really... It's all new."

"That man is head over heels for you. He's staring at you right now like he wants to eat you up."

Dawn had stopped talking, waiting for our attention so she could make her proclamation. Everyone else had gone silent too, and Granny's words echoed over the deck.

I tried to think of something to say, but all that came out was "um..."

"I think I should have dinner first," Graham said as though responding to a completely innocuous statement.

After some light and only slightly uncomfortable laughter, Dawn said, "We have chicken, hamburgers, and hot dogs for the grill, but I wanted to see who wants what."

We all gave responses, and she tallied up the right amount of each item. "I'll throw on some extra too, of course," she added before turning to go inside.

"Would you like some help?" Graham asked.

"Oh, no. You're a guest."

Felicity started to follow Dawn. "I'll help."

"That's probably not a good idea," I said. Felicity and her mom working together on things tended not to end well.

Dawn nodded. "You will not. I don't need you meddling. If you insist on doing something, you can refill everyone's drinks."

Felicity glared at me, and I knew I was going to pay for that.

When we were all seated with our plates and Granny had said grace, Felicity gave me an evil grin. "Did you hurt yourself, Avery?"

"What? No."

"Huh. I noticed you seemed to be having trouble sitting down."

Holy shit, she didn't. "No… um… the dogs. They were under the table, and I was trying not to step on them. That's all."

"Really?" She glanced pointedly at the dogs who were frisking out on the lawn. "I thought maybe Graham had—"

"Felicity." Everyone jumped at Carter's sharp tone.

"See," Granny said. "I told you he was the right one. He seems all mild and easygoing, but he's not afraid to call her out when she goes too far."

"I have not—"

"I didn't mean—"

Felicity and Carter's words ran over each other. Then Felicity gave me a sickeningly sweet smile. "Those dogs really can be trouble when they get underfoot."

As if to deliberately make the evening more impossible, Graham picked up his hot dog and wrapped his lips around it. Did he really have to choose a hot dog?

"Is something wrong, Avery?" Felicity asked, still using her sweet Southern girl voice.

"What? No." I was suddenly sweating. despite the cool evening breeze.

"You aren't eating."

"Oh, I was just… thinking."

Granny snorted. "Probably praying for his man to take him home, so he won't have to deal with more of this insanity."

That made Graham nearly choke on his hot dog, which only made the situation worse.

Wait a minute. Hadn't he said he wanted chicken when Dawn asked? I scowled at Felicity. This was her doing. I was sure of it. I glanced around. Carter had chicken on his plate when he'd asked for a hot dog. She'd switched them, and Graham was too polite to complain and Carter probably didn't want to get into it with her.

"I thought maybe something had caught your attention," Felicity said.

"Felicity, leave him alone so he can eat," Dawn said.

"But he's not eating, that's why I was concerned."

"I regret that you're too old for me to send you to your room, and I doubt you have that kind of relationship with Carter."

She frowned. "What kind?"

"The kind where he spanks you," Dawn said.

Carter's eyes went wide and he made a strangled noise like some chicken had lodged in his throat.

Granny pushed herself up from her chair. "Dammit, Dawn, you may have killed him now, and she'll never find another man as nice as he is."

"What are you doing?" Dawn asked as Granny moved behind Carter.

"Giving him that Heimlich thingy so he doesn't choke to death."

"No," Carter managed to get out between sputtering coughs. "I'm okay."

I looked over at Graham. His face was nearly as red as Carter's.

"Do you need to get out of here?" I whispered to him.

"No. We… we better stay."

"I promise it's not always this bad." That was a lie, but I didn't want him convinced his son had married into a family of lunatics.

"Avery and Graham, why don't you tell us the whole story of how you got together?" Dawn smiled brightly as if she hadn't just nearly killed her son-in-law and embarrassed the rest of us.

"Um…" *Think of something. Anything that doesn't have to do with kinky sex.*

Carter, having finally stopped coughing, tried to rescue us. "Like my dad said, they met at the wedding and hit it off, so they decided to go out."

"The bride's best friend and the father of the groom. There has to be more to the story. It's like something from a movie."

"I didn't know he was Carter's dad when I met him," I blurted out. "Once I realized who he was, I thought maybe I shouldn't ask him out, but at the reception, I realized he felt the same way, and so here we are." Asking him out wasn't exactly what I'd wanted to do, but I wasn't going to tell them I'd wanted to drag him to the nearest empty room and beg him to fuck me.

Dawn frowned. "I still think you're leaving a lot out."

"Only things that would be impolite to discuss at the dinner table," Graham said.

Carter started going red again. "We, um… we know all we need to."

"For now," Dawn said, her tone ominous.

"For good," Graham insisted, using the authoritative tone that was so fucking hot I had to quickly think of horrible things like poorly dyed hair and clumpy mascara to keep my cock from getting excited.

"Fine, but you two are no fun," Felicity said.

Granny winked at me. "I bet they're a whole lotta fun when no one else is around."

Carter groaned and dropped his head into his hands. I wanted to offer him another drink. He'd certainly chosen a challenging family to join.

For the rest of dinner, the conversation only skirted the edges of embarrassing or inappropriate. When most of our plates were empty, Dawn glanced around. "Is everyone ready for lemon cake?"

"Yes, please!" I said. Then in a stage whisper I told Graham, "Once you taste this cake, you'll think the evening was worth it."

Dawn brought each of us a piece, and the sound Graham made when he had his first bite was even better than the cake itself. "This is amazing."

Dawn beamed. "Thank you."

"It really is," I said. "Thank you for making it for me."

"Any time. You know I love making you happy."

I was happy, but not just because of the cake. I was surrounded by people who loved me, people who were more of a family than my biological one had ever been. And now I had Graham too. He squeezed my leg, and I let myself watch as he brought another bite to his mouth. I took his hand and squeezed back. I'd been content knowing I had Felicity and her mom and Granny, but Graham was something I'd needed for a long time. I was so lucky to have found him.

***

Monday morning came way too soon. I didn't want Graham to leave, but I was starting to worry because kissing goodbye had turned into fucking goodbye, and Graham had said he had to leave early.

"Weren't you supposed to be on the road already?" I asked as I drew circles on his chest.

He sighed. "Yeah, but I was just thinking I could probably manage another day working from here."

I sat up and looked down at him. "I won't let you screw up your business for me. We'll talk tomorrow night and—"

He flipped me under him and pinned my wrists to the mattress. "I don't want to only see you on a screen for the next ten days."

I bit my lip to hold in a whimper. I loved him going all dominant like this. "I wish you could come back this weekend."

"Me too, but I have to meet with developers and look at some properties."

I stuck my lip out. I hadn't meant to be bratty, but going ten days from the wedding until he'd come to visit had felt like torture.

"Avery." He was warning me not to push further.

"Sorry, Daddy."

"I certainly could find time to spank you, even if I have to cancel my first meeting."

I sucked in my breath, and my cock responded as Graham thrust against me.

"You like that idea."

"Maybe." I laughed as I arched into him, rubbing my cock against his.

"I have another idea I think you'll like." He rolled to his side and propped himself on his elbow.

"What is that?"

"I want to fuck you bare. I want to see my cum dripping from your ass."

I groaned, barely resisting reaching for my cock. "Can we?"

He held my gaze. "If we do, then it's just me and you, no fucking anyone else."

"I don't want anyone but you. I haven't since our first night."

He smiled. "I feel the same way, boy. I want you to get tested as soon as possible. Today, if you can. I will too, and when I come back, I'll fuck you full of my cum."

"Yes, please."

He took my cock in his hand and stroked me. "I can see you do like that idea."

"I do."

"It's too bad you won't be able to do anything about this, though." He teased my cock, stroking it slowly. "You're not to come unless I ask you to when we're talking."

Just those few lazy strokes had gotten me fully hard and ready for another round. This was going to be a long week. "Yes, Daddy."

"I expect you to do better this time."

"I'll be good. I promise."

"If you are, you'll not only get to feel me inside you bare, we'll work some more on stretching your tight ass, because eventually, I want you to take all this." He held up a hand and wiggled his fingers.

Holy shit. "Yes, Daddy!"

"I would hate to have to keep that reward from you because you couldn't obey."

"I can, Daddy."

"I know you can." He swung his legs over the side of the bed and stood. "I'm going to shower now, and you're going to make coffee and pour me some for the road. Once I've left, you need to shower and get ready for work. I don't want you to be late."

"Yes, Daddy." Heat filled my face. "Um… Graham?"

"What is it, baby?"

"I really do like when you tell me what to do like that, not just for sex. I mean, I like it for sex too, but this is good."

He smiled. "I like it too. Next time I'm here, we'll talk more about the boundaries we want to set, okay?"

"Yes, Daddy."

I watched his gorgeous ass as he walked to the bathroom. Then I hurried to the kitchen. My daddy needed coffee.

CHAPTER SIX

AVERY

I'd longed for Graham every day since he'd gone back to Charlotte. Now it was finally the day we'd be reunited. I should've been ready to explode with excitement, but ever since I'd left the house this morning, things had been going wrong. First, I'd tripped on a rut in the sidewalk and spilled my coffee all over myself. Midmorning, we had a power failure while I was in the middle of blowing out a new client's hair. After lunch, I dropped an eyeshadow palette, and it broke apart all over the floor. Then I had to fix the toilet in one of the bathrooms when it overflowed. I wasn't otherwise occupied, because one of my appointments was a no-show.

The only thing keeping me from running out of work screaming was texting Graham. Every time I told him about one more shitty thing that had happened, he sent hearts, emojis, and hints about what he would do to me later. If I survived these next three hours, I could go home to him, and he would make me feel better. So I knew that, despite all this, I was a lucky man.

Carol, one of the other stylists, stuck her head into the break room. "The Wilson bridal party is here."

I like doing makeovers. I like doing makeovers, I chanted to myself. I'd had the "pleasure" of meeting this particular bridezilla and her giggling posse a few months ago. I was not looking forward to having them tell me what they wanted and then refusing to listen to my suggestions of what would actually look good on them.

"I'll be right there." I sent Graham one more text telling him to pray for me, downed a glass of water, and went to face my fate.

***

"Graham!" I called when I stepped into his condo.

He didn't answer, so I headed into the living room. He was there on the couch. He put his laptop down, stood, and faced me.

I sucked in my breath as he looked me up and down, heat in his eyes.

"Daddy?"

He took my bag from my shoulder and set it down. "I have an idea for how to make you forget all about your bad day, but if you'd rather have dinner first or—"

"No." I licked my lips. "I like your ideas. I like them a lot."

"Bend over the back of the couch," he said.

"Yes, Daddy."

At first I'd been slightly startled by him jumping right into role play, but then I'd realized this was exactly what I needed. He was doing this for me, to relax me, and that got me hard in record time. I got into position, sticking my ass out and shaking it, which earned me the slap I expected. "Ow!"

"Hush. Good boys stay still and quiet while their Daddy works them over."

Oh my God. "Yes, Daddy."

He unbuckled my pants and pushed them and my briefs down until they pooled around my ankles.

"Step out and kick them away," he commanded.

I did and then I looked over my shoulder to see what he was doing. I really wanted to know where this was going. Hopefully toward something nice and thick stuffed up my ass.

"Head down."

"Daddy," I whined, knowing I was pushing him.

He slapped my ass hard, making me cry out. Then he hit me again in the same spot. "Fuck, that hurts."

"It's supposed to, and if I have to do it again, my boy won't get to come tonight."

Shit. I really, really needed to come. Graham had mercy on me one of the nights we Skyped, talking me through an incredible orgasm, but other than that, I hadn't come in ten days. "I'll be good, Daddy."

"I hope so. Now stick that hot ass out and arch your back."

That I had no problem doing, but I jumped when he drizzled cold lube onto me, letting it slide down my crack.

"Is that cold, boy?"

"Fuck, yes."

"Boy?"

His tone made me shiver. "Yes, it's cold, Daddy."

"Better." He slid his fingers through the lube and circled my hole, teasing, making me want to beg. I bit my lip to hide my need.

"Stop holding back, boy. I want to hear you beg."

He always knew what I was feeling, even when he couldn't see my face. "Daddy, please."

"Tell me what you need."

"I need you to fuck me."

He chuckled. "We're a long way from that."

I groaned. "Daddy."

"Boy, you're asking for a spanking and a cock cage."

"Oh, my God."

He leaned close. "Would you let me do that to you?"

"I… I don't know."

"It's okay. You don't have to decide now, and you don't have to do it ever. I just thought about how hot it would be."

"Yeah," I whispered the word as I imagined it.

"My boy all locked up, unable to get off without his daddy."

"Fuck." He made it sound incredible.

"Of course you're so good you obey without it, don't you?"

"I want to. I want to be good."

"You are." He pushed a few fingers into me, working them deep, twisting them and fucking me with them until I was panting and fighting the urge to fuck back into them.

He stroked my back. "See, you're so good. You do just what Daddy tells you to." He wrapped a hand around my cock and gave it a slow pull. "You're learning to hold off longer, aren't you?"

I whimpered. "I don't know if I… if I can…"

He let go of my cock and pulled his fingers from my ass. I couldn't decide if I was disappointed or grateful he stopped so I didn't come without permission.

"Face me and kneel."

I scrambled to obey. I could see his hard cock pressing against his dress pants. I wanted to please him, to make him feel as good as I did. "Daddy, can I suck your cock?"

"Not now, boy." He reached into a bag that sat on the floor behind him and pulled out a blue dildo. It was a little smaller around than his cock but longer, with a pair of huge fake balls at the base.

He brushed it over my lips. "Suck on this. Get it good and wet so it's ready for your ass." I could feel precum dripping from my cock as I licked my lips and opened my mouth.

I reached for the dildo, but he stepped away. "Hands behind your back."

I did as he said, and he pushed the dildo into my mouth, giving me only a little at first. The tip was smooth but there were ridges along the shaft.

"That's good, boy. Coat it in your spit."

I sucked it sloppily, and he pushed it farther in. "Open up. I want you to take it all."

I wasn't sure I could, but I wanted to. I wanted to please him so badly.

He pushed it deeper, and I gagged, tears coming to my eyes. He pulled back. "You're trying so hard. I'm proud of you, boy."

"I want to try again, Daddy. I can do it." I was determined to, because it was what he wanted from me, and I wanted to please him. It made me feel powerful. Yes, I was on my knees. Yes, he was pushing a long dildo down my throat, but I was free to say no, and I was giving him pleasure.

"It's okay, boy. We can stop now."

I shook my head and leaned forward to lick the spit-slick tip of the dildo.

Graham growled and slid it into my mouth, fucking me with it. Then he pushed it deeper. I swallowed around it. He pulled back and then pushed it in again, all the way this time. I gagged around it, and he pulled it out quickly, but I'd done it, I'd taken it all.

His eyes were wide, and he had a hand over the bulge in his pants. "That was amazing, boy. Seeing you with this down your throat almost made me come."

I grinned. "Thank you, Daddy."

"Turn around and get on your hands and knees. I want to see that gorgeous ass again."

I did as he asked and immediately felt the tip of the dildo press against my ass, feeling glad Graham had already lubed and stretched it.

"I'm going to fill you up with this, and then I'll have you get my cock all slicked up too."

"Oh my God. Are you…?"

"I'm going to fuck you with this." He pushed the dildo in and the sting made my breath catch. "And then I'm going to put my cock in you too, right alongside it. I'll stretch your ass so good, so nice and wide."

"Holy fuck. Daddy. Please."

"You want that?"

"Yes. I want you to fill me up like that, split me open."

"I will. You'll be so full you'll think you can't take it."

"I can, Daddy. I'm a good boy."

"You are." He stroked my ass as he pushed the dildo deeper. "But that doesn't mean you have to do this if it's too much. You can stop me any time."

"Thank you, Daddy. You take such good care of me."

I glanced back at him. He was watching my ass swallow the dildo as he worked it all the way in. The look on his face showed wonder, lust, pride, and maybe something more. I shuddered and let my head drop down as the silicone balls pressed against me. I felt so full already. "Fuck."

"Breathe, boy."

I tried to drag air into my lungs, but they felt constricted. My pulse pounded in my ears. He was really going to fuck me with his cock and a dildo. It was going to hurt, but I wanted it so badly I could come just thinking about it.

"Daddy?" My voice was hoarse and strained.

He rubbed my back. "Tell me what you need, boy."

"I want to do this, but I need to come."

He chuckled, the sound low and dark. "Yes, you do."

"Please let me come so… so I…"

"Say it, boy. I may not grant your wish, but I will always listen to you."

"I'm afraid I won't be able to hold back if you're stretching my ass like you want to, and I won't enjoy it as much if I'm fighting not to come."

"So you want me to take the edge off. Is that right?"

I bit my lip, considering telling him to never mind, but that was what I'd been thinking. "Yes, Daddy."

He pulled the dildo from my ass, and it made an obscene sound as it popped free. "Turn around, boy."

I knelt at his feet, my cock jutting out in front of me, red and needy as I waited to see if he'd give me what I'd asked for.

He stroked my cheek and ran his fingers along my jaw. "I love watching you struggle, boy. You're so beautiful when you suffer, and you come so hard for me when I make you hold off."

I started to speak, but he laid a finger over my lips. "Not yet."

He walked all the way around me and I could feel him watching me. "Will you really enjoy this more if you aren't having to hold back?"

"Um… I think so. Yes."

He moved back in front of me and raised his brows. "Are you sure?"

Was I, or was I just so desperate I'd say anything for a chance to come? "I think so."

"Boy, do you trust me?"

I nodded. I still didn't understand how I'd known instinctively that he would never hurt me, but I did, and he'd proven me right many times.

"Will you let me make this decision for you?"

"Yes, Daddy." The answer came automatically.

"Thank you, boy. I'm going to put a cock ring on you, and you're going to wait. You're resisting, because you've had a hard day, but I know how good it will be for you if I make you wait."

"Daddy," I whined.

"Do you need my belt first? Because your pretty ass will hurt a lot more if I spank you first."

"No, Daddy. I'll be good."

"I know you will. Now I want you on the bed on your back."

"Yes, Daddy." I tried to stand, but I was dizzy and my legs shook. He took hold of my arms.

"Can you walk, baby?"

"If you help me."

He took hold of my chin and forced me to look at him. "Avery, are you okay? You remember your safeword, right?"

"It's red, Daddy, and I'm all right. I need this so much. I'm just a little scared."

"Of it hurting too much?"

"I… Yeah."

"It's okay. I'll go slow, and I'll stop right away if you ask me to. I won't love you any less if you don't want this."

I sucked in my breath. Love? Had I heard that right? "Graham?"

"Not now." He scooped me into his arms and carried me to the bed. When he laid me on my back, I pulled my legs up, opening myself for him.

He got a cock ring from his bag and put it on me. Then he held out the dildo.

"Fuck yourself with this, and don't stop unless I tell you to."

"Oh my God."

"Boy?"

"I'm sorry. Yes, sir, Daddy."

I brought the dildo between my legs and pushed it into me, groaning as I did.

"That's right, boy, all the way in."

I pushed deeper until I felt like it was impossibly far inside me. I tilted my hips, and it grazed my prostate, making me cry out.

"Feels good, doesn't it?"

"Yes," I cried.

"Keep going. In and out. Nice and slow." He straddled my shoulders as he spoke. "Now suck me while you fuck yourself. Get me nice and wet, so I can wreck your ass. You're going to take me and that dildo, and you're going to love it."

I whimpered as he brushed his cock against my lips the way he had with the dildo a few moments before. I curled forward so I could take him in. I needed this, needed him to choke me with his cock while I worked the dildo into myself. My cock ached. A puddle of precum had already gathered on my stomach.

I would've begged Daddy again to let me come, but his cock was deep in my throat, and all I could do was moan around it.

"Fuck, that's good, boy." He worked his hips, fucking my mouth, more gentle than he'd been with the dildo. My throat hurt, but I didn't care. I wanted to hurt for him. I'd missed him so much this week.

Finally he pulled out of me and wiped my drool-covered face with the sheet. "Keep the dildo still inside you, baby."

I did, and he knelt between my legs and put his hand over mine. "I've got it now. You hold your legs."

With his other hand, he picked up the lube, but instead of squirting it on his cock, he drizzled it over mine. Then he gripped me tight and slid his hand up and down.

"Daddy!"

"Relax, boy."

"I can't. You know I can't."

He slapped my ass hard. "Don't tell me what I know."

"Please. I'm sorry, Daddy. Please." Tears stung my eyes.

He kept stroking me, slow but relentless.

"Why are you pushing me so hard?"

"Because you need it."

The tears began to roll down my cheeks then. "I do. How did you know?"

"I'm not sure. I just do. Now let me give it to you."

I drew in a shaky breath, tears still spilling over. "Yes, Daddy. Please give me what I need."

He kissed the inside of my knees. "You're such a good boy."

A few moments later, he let go of my aching cock, squirted more lube into his hand, and used it to coat his shaft.

"Put your hands over your head," he demanded as he pulled the dildo from my body.

I did, even though I wanted to touch him so badly I nearly begged for it.

"I'm going to fuck you bare now, boy. Is that okay?"

I sucked in my breath as I nodded frantically. We'd both gotten back negative test results, and I couldn't wait to feel him inside me with nothing between us.

He gripped my thighs as he eased in. "So good, boy. So hot and tight."

I groaned, wanting to beg for more but knowing he would set the pace. Finally he pushed all the way in and then began to move. "I'm going to fill your ass with my cum, boy."

"Yes, please, Daddy!"

"I want to see it dripping out of you."

"Oh, God." I worked my hips, desperate for more, but he pulled out.

"It's time to stretch that ass some more."

"Please."

He rubbed more lube over the dildo, then pushed it back in. After fucking me with it for a moment, he left it partway in and slid a slick finger around the rim of my stretched hole before pushing it into me alongside the dildo.

"Daddy, I—"

"Shhh. Relax and just let it happen."

"I… I'll try."

"You can do this, boy. I know you can."

He added another finger, and it hurt. God, it hurt, but I wanted it. The pain was somehow making me need to come even more. "Daddy, please."

"Please what?"

"Your cock. I want your cock in me."

"I know, boy. Do you really think you're ready?"

He held my gaze, and I bit my lip. Would I ever really be ready? "If you think I am, Daddy."

He smiled. "You are. You're my good boy who's ready for my cock."

He added more lube and then positioned himself between my legs. He pulled the dildo almost all the way out, and I felt the tip of his cock brush against me. Then he was pushing in. There was pressure and pain. It stung so badly my eyes watered.

"Fuck, that's tight. Are you really going to fit?"

"I'll fit. Just be patient."

"Yes, Daddy."

Entering me seemed to take forever. I tried not to fight it, but there was a moment when I really thought I'd split in two. Then he was there, all the way inside me along with the dildo. He made shallow thrusts that were messy and uncoordinated, but at some point it went from painful to the hottest thing ever.

"Daddy! Daddy, please! I need to come. Please let me!" My balls were going to explode. I couldn't hold back anymore.

He looked down to where my ass was stretched around him and the toy. "So hot. You've done so good taking all this."

He pulled the dildo and his cock all the way out. When he pushed back in, it was just him. He unfastened the cock ring. "Come for me, boy."

He fucked me hard and deep, and I cried out, working my hips, trying to take him into me as far as I could. "Yes, fuck me, Daddy."

In seconds I was coming, my release burning through me in nearly painful spasms. Graham was right behind me. He dug his fingers into my thighs and jerked his hips against my ass. Then I felt the hot flood of his cum.

The way Graham looked at me when he emptied himself stole what little breath I had left. I wanted to say something, but my brain had shut down.

After taking a moment to recover, he pulled out and lay down next to me. I reached down to touch the wetness on my inner thighs. "I can feel your cum sliding out of me."

"Fuck. I need to see." I opened my legs, and he shifted position. "That's so hot. Your ass is all stretched out, and my cum is all over you."

I smiled. "I love how it feels, Daddy."

He touched the edge of my hole, and I flinched. "Too sore?"

"Kinda, but you don't have to stop."

"I'm already getting hard again just looking at you. That shouldn't be possible this fast." He slid his fingers through the stickiness and brought them to my mouth.

Holy fuck, I would never have thought I'd like this, but as I licked them clean, my cock filled again.

"Fuck some of it back into me, Daddy."

He growled as he rose up on his knees and pushed his cock into me again. "This feels incredible, boy."

"Can you come again, Daddy?"

"I don't know."

"I want you to. I want it on me this time. I want to be covered in your cum, inside and out."

"You're insatiable, boy."

"Only for you, Daddy."

He pulled out and stretched out over me, lining our cocks up so they rubbed against each other as he flexed his hips. I held onto his waist as I bucked up, adding more friction. We were slick with lube and cum, and it was glorious. His movements grew more and more erratic.

"Boy, tell me what you want, talk to me."

"I want to make you come again." I held on tight and worked my hips as fast as I could. I wasn't sure where all the energy had come from. I'd been sure I was thoroughly sated until I felt his cum slide out of me. "Please, Daddy. I love your cum. I want more of it."

"Goddammit, boy, you're so good to me."

"I want to be, Daddy. Come for me, Daddy. Come all over me. I love being messy, claimed, marked by you."

"Holy fuck!" He tensed and then I felt the hot splash of his seed on my stomach. The sensation sent me over too. When we finished, he rolled off me and onto his back. I looked down my body. "Wow. I'm a complete mess."

He grunted as he shifted onto his side. "What you are is beautiful."

I whimpered. The way he was looking at me was so hot, and I still wanted more, but— "I can't go again. I just can't."

"Baby." He ran his hand through the mess on my stomach. "Neither can I, but you are the sexiest man I've ever seen."

Heat rushed to my face at the compliment. How could I feel shy with him after what we'd just done?

He caressed me and then brought his fingers to his mouth, eyes going closed as he sucked them.

"So hot, Daddy."

"I love tasting us together."

"Kiss me."

He did, his tongue sliding along mine. He licked at my lips and then tugged the bottom one with his teeth. My cock wanted to stir, but I was thoroughly spent.

Graham smiled at me when he pulled back. "I'm going to get you some water and then clean you up."

"Thank you, Daddy. That was just what I needed."

He smiled. "I thought it would be."

CHAPTER SEVEN

GRAHAM

After all I'd put him through, my boy needed to rest, so I ordered a pizza for us, and we spent the rest of the night snuggling. Avery didn't mention my use of the word "love," and I decided it was best to let that go for now. We didn't talk anymore about boundaries for our Daddy/boy play, but one more day of waiting on that wasn't going to hurt.

I had lunch with all three of my kids and dealt with some paperwork while Avery was at the salon the next day. When he got home, I fed him grilled chicken and salad filled with fresh vegetables from the farmer's market. I'd originally planned to take him out, but he'd been so thrilled by me cooking for him the last time I'd visited that I decided to do it again.

"This chicken is amazing," he said, his smile all the thanks I'd ever need.

"I'm glad you like it. After we finish, you get to decide if you want to go out for dessert or cocktails or just stay here."

He beamed at me. "Thank you, Daddy."

"I'm very proud of my boy. You were so good for me this week, you only touched yourself when I told you to, and I want to reward you."

"Giving me yourself bare and the dildo too was like the best reward ever."

I grinned. "How did I get this lucky?"

Avery squeezed my hand. "I feel like I'm the lucky one."

I had to swallow around the lump in my throat. I wanted to tell him I loved him right then, but I didn't want to scare him. I'd tell him eventually. I was reasonably sure he felt the same way, but I wasn't ready to find out.

When we'd finished eating and had cleaned up, I realized Avery had been much less chatty than usual. "Are you all right, baby? Did you have a bad day?"

"No, a good day actually, but I was really glad I get to stand up to do my job."

I couldn't help but smile. "Just how sore are you?"

"Not too sore to let you have me again, Daddy."

I growled. "Don't tempt me, boy. Your ass needs a rest after last night."

"My mouth doesn't."

I narrowed my eyes. "You didn't answer my question."

He suddenly became very interested in the view from the balcony. "I had a good day."

"But something is bothering you."

"Um… well… could we talk a minute before we go out, you know, without any role play?"

I hoped that didn't mean something really was wrong. "Sure we can. I can be whatever you need, a Daddy, a Dom, or just Graham."

He sighed. "You're amazing."

"I care about you. That's all." I stroked his cheek, and he leaned into my touch.

"Could we snuggle while we talk? I think that would make it easier."

"Of course." He squealed in surprise when I picked him up, but as I carried him to the sofa, he relaxed in my arms and pressed his lips to my neck.

I wanted him on my lap, but that felt too much like what a daddy would do, so I settled him next to me and put my arm around him. "I intended for us to talk more about boundaries before now. I'm sorry we haven't."

He shook his head. "That's not your fault. I could've asked before now, but I think part of the reason I didn't was that being your boy feels so comfortable, and it's been working to use each other's names as a signal to step back, or at least it seems like it has."

I nodded. "I feel like that too, and I've always taken you calling me Graham as a sign that you want me to respond differently than I would if you called me Daddy. But if you want something else or more clear boundaries, we can figure that out."

"The thing is I really don't, but I feel like I should. That's why I brought it up."

I pulled him tighter to me and kissed the top of his head. "There aren't any shoulds outside of consent and respect."

"I guess not, but it's hard not to wonder why I feel like I do. At first I thought I'd only want to play like this during sex, but when the lines started to blur for us, I loved it. I didn't want to stop being your boy just because we weren't in bed. I realized I haven't even been thinking about stopping and starting at all. It's just like we are who we are with each other, and part of that is Daddy and boy."

84

I was so awed by him that it took me a moment to put words together. "Avery, that's… Thank you so much for telling me that. I never thought you'd feel like that. I never thought I would, either. I even told you I didn't want this to be a lifestyle thing, because I never had. I didn't think that would suit me, but with you it all seems natural."

Avery shifted so he was looking at me. He took my hands and looked down at our intertwined fingers. "I wondered at first if we didn't know how to relate to each other any other way, because we'd only had that one weekend together. But that's not it, is it?"

I shook my head. "I don't think so. I think this is just what's right for us. I'm still not sure it will be all the time. I think there are going to be moments, maybe even whole days or weeks, that one or both of us will want to step aside from those roles."

"Me too," Avery said, looking up at me. "But I like what we're doing. I like when you make choices for me. I like when you tell me what I should do next. I think that if we were together all the time, I wouldn't want you always doing that, but some of the time… yeah."

His cheeks were an adorable pink. I reached up and stroked them with my thumbs. "Do you want to keep on using each other's names if we need to step back from our roles?"

He nodded. "Yeah, I do."

I pulled him onto my lap then. "I know I'm going to screw up at some point, boy. Just know I want so much to do what's right. You can always use your safeword if you need to stop role-playing, and I'm not getting it, okay?"

He snuggled in and nuzzled me. "I know, Daddy. And you can use it too, if you need to stop."

"Oh, baby. Thank you. You're so fucking perfect."

"I trust you more than I've ever trusted anyone other than Felicity. Maybe that's crazy, but it's true."

"I keep thinking all this should feel crazy, but it doesn't. It just feels right."

"So right."

***

I spent every one of the next few weekends in Asheville. Avery and I went to dinner a few times. We heard a band one of the other stylists from Oasis Asheville was in. He introduced me to a few more food trucks and some of his favorite beers, but we spent most of our time in the condo. I cooked for him. We talked, learning more about each other's past, more about our dreams for the future, and all about every inch of our bodies and all the things we both liked such as riding crops, love bites, and that damned amazing remote-controlled plug.

A few days before my next visit to Asheville, Leo called to say he'd talked more with the owner of Thrust, and he was ready to seriously consider putting in an offer. He had plans to meet the owner and manager on Friday afternoon and then spend the evening at the club. Leo told me I didn't have to go with him, but I could tell he really wanted my opinion.

I locked my office door and called Avery, hoping he wasn't going to be upset that I wanted to make an alteration in our plans.

"Graham, hey, what's up?"

"Have you got time to talk?"

"Yeah, I just got home from work."

"I need to ask you a few things about the weekend." I should've just said it, but I was stalling, because I was nervous.

"Do you want to Skype instead?"

"Not yet. If I see you, it'll distract me too much."

Avery laughed. "I can distract you without any visuals."

"You could, but you won't because you're a good boy."

"I am, Daddy," he purred, emphasizing the last word. My cock responded as he'd no doubt known it would.

"Watch it, boy."

"So is this a good thing about the weekend? You're still coming Friday, right?"

Just say it. I took a deep breath. "Yes, I'll still be there Friday, but you remember me telling you about my friend Leo?"

"Of course I do. He helped you build a new life, and he owns a club, and you went to Italy with him?"

I nodded even though he couldn't see me. "That's right. He's thinking about buying a club in Asheville."

"Thrust?"

"Yeah, that's the one. How'd you know?"

"I'd heard that the owner, Allen, wants to sell it. He's moving somewhere. Maybe to California."

"Yeah, I think that's right. So what do you think of the place?"

"I like it. It's safe and comfortable. I was actually planning to go there the night of the wedding."

"But you met me." I had to force myself not to growl at the idea of him having left the wedding to find someone else.

"I did. I found exactly what I needed."

"That's right, boy. Don't you forget it."

"No chance of that." The purr was back in his voice.

"So you think Leo should take a look?"

"Definitely. I'd love to know someone trustworthy is taking it over. It's gotten more crowded in the last year, and tourists wander in, especially on weekend nights. That's really the only thing I don't like."

"So it might need an expansion or a long-time members area or something."

"Yeah, but he should look at it for sure. I know a few of the regulars, so I could connect him with them if he wants their perspective."

"Perfect. He wants to come up this weekend and check it out."

"Oh."

I could hear his disappointment, but I kept going. "He wants to meet you."

"Shit. I… Um… The two of you were… are… What are you to each other now?"

"Friends, Avery. That's all. Even if I hadn't promised to be exclusive with you, I wouldn't be fucking Leo. We haven't been more than friends for a long time."

"Oh, that's… Thank you for telling me. I'm just not sure how I feel about meeting him."

I wasn't going to force this, no matter how much I wanted Leo to meet the man who'd stolen my heart. "If you're not ready, that's completely understandable."

"But it's not fair. You've already met my best friend."

"Yes, but that was a little different."

Avery laughed. "Just a little, but being your daughter-in-law wouldn't have stopped her from warning me off if she thought it necessary."

"I'm sure it wouldn't." Felicity wasn't one to hold back her opinions.

"How much does he know about us?"

I was tempted to lie, but he deserved my honesty. "Basically everything."

"The Daddy kink too?"

"Yes, but only because he already knew it was one of my preferences. He's seen me play with boys at his club." *Please don't be mad.*

Several seconds passed, then he said, "I want to be annoyed, but I probably would've told Felicity if she wasn't related to you."

"I still should've asked you first. I'm sorry."

"No, it's good that you have someone you can talk to."

I finally exhaled fully when he said that. "Thank you."

"You're welcome, Daddy. I want you to be happy, and I trust you."

"Good. I trust you too. Leo proposed dinner on Friday and then going to the club together. But if you don't want to go, I can stay long enough to give my opinion and then come home to you."

"You realize if we go together, I might see people I've played with."

I automatically clenched my fists and then had to remind myself I was a mature adult, not a jealous caveman. "I figured that would be the case."

"And you won't mind?"

"Not unless you decide you'd rather play with them. Would you mind if you met some of the boys I'd played with?"

"I want to say no, but…"

"Fine. I'll be jealous as hell, but that's ridiculous, and I won't act on it."

"Yeah, same."

"How do you feel about going with me?"

He sighed. "Okay, I guess. If we're… If this is real then we need to meet each other's friends eventually. But… um… do you want to play at the club or just observe?"

"I'd love to play with you, if you want that, but if not, that's okay too." I paced in front of my office window, anxious for his answer.

"What would you want to do?"

Once again, I decided to go for full honesty. "I want to spank you while people watch. I want to show off what a good boy you are."

I heard Avery suck in his breath. "Um… I…"

"I want them to hear my hand crack against your ass, see you squirm, hear you cry out for more."

"Oh my God, Daddy."

"Do you want that too?"

"I… Yeah, I do."

"Then I'll give it to you."

"Wow. That would be…" He took a shaky breath.

"You're hard, aren't you? Just thinking about being exposed like that, about needing to be good so you make your daddy proud, has you ready to come."

"Yes, Daddy."

"Are you alone?"

"Uh-huh."

"Take your cock out. You're going to jerk off, and I'm going to listen. I want to hear everything."

"You can watch if you want to, Daddy."

I bit back a groan. "I'm still at work, and I don't want to risk it."

"You're in your office, listening to me? That's so hot."

I chuckled. "You're such a slutty boy."

"I am. My cock is out now, Daddy. I'm getting some lube on my hand, and now I'm…" He groaned. "Working myself."

"Fist it tightly, so hard it almost hurts."

Avery sucked in his breath.

"Good boy. Now stroke yourself hard and fast. I don't have long, and I need to hear you come before I get off the phone."

His breathing picked up, and I could hear the slick, sliding sound of his hand working over his cock.

"So good. It feels so good, Daddy."

"I know it does. Touch your balls too. Tug on them. Work yourself over like I was watching, like you wanted me to see what you could do."

"Daddy," he whimpered. "So good. So close."

"Give it to me. Come on, boy."

He was moaning now, and I could hear him shifting against the bed.

"Tug harder."

"Oh God, Daddy. I'm coming."

"Yes, boy. Come for me."

He shouted, and I could imagine him arching off the bed, eyes shut, face slowly going slack as he pumped out his release.

"You're such a good boy for giving that to Daddy."

He whimpered.

"You love being a slutty boy and getting off while I'm at work, don't you?"

"I do, Daddy."

I sank back into my chair, my legs too shaky to keep me upright. "I'm going to love showing you off on Friday."

"Yes, please. I didn't even know I wanted that until you said it, but wow, it sounds so hot."

I smiled. "I love how eager you are, but no touching yourself until I'm there."

"Yes, Daddy." He sounded so disappointed.

"I've got to go, but we'll talk tomorrow, and I'll see you Friday."

"I miss you, Graham."

"I miss you too, baby."

***

Friday dragged by. I had an interminable meeting with an investor who didn't seem to know what he wanted and whose lawyer was an arrogant piece of shit. Then my laptop decided to pitch a fit, and the office lunch delivery got mixed up, so I ended up with nothing but an apple to eat. By the time I was headed out the door, I was so ready to get to Asheville, I didn't know how I was going to stand two hours in summer weekend traffic.

Thrust's current owner, Allen, had managed to score us reservations at Casa Lucas, one of the hottest places in Asheville. Avery was going to be thrilled. He'd told me he'd never been, because it was impossible to get a weekend night reservation, even months in advance. Allen played soccer with the owner, though, so he'd been able to work it out.

I was looking forward to everything about this night. I had some surprises for Avery, and I intended to get him all worked up before we went out. I'd tease him as much as I could at dinner without embarrassing him in front of Leo. Then, as soon as I'd gotten a feel for the atmosphere at Thrust, I was going to redden his ass until he was dying to come, not that I'd let that happen while people watched. His orgasms were for me and only me. He'd have to wait until we were in a private room to finally get relief.

CHAPTER EIGHT

AVERY

I hurried through cleaning my workstation so I could get to Graham's condo. He'd told me I was going to love dinner, but he wouldn't tell me where we were eating. He also said he had some other surprises for me. Considering his last surprise was a vibrating butt plug, I was a bit worried what he meant. Was he going to find another way to torment me tonight? I wasn't sure whether I hoped for that or didn't.

I let myself in when I got to the condo.

"Avery?" Graham called from somewhere in the back.

"It's me."

"Come to the bedroom."

I liked the sound of that. I set my bag down and raced down the hall. "What are you going to torture me with tonight?"

He grinned and held up a bright pink jockstrap with a lace panel in the front.

"Oh wow. I thought you might have brought the plug for me again or something worse."

Graham raised his brows. "What were you thinking of that would be worse?"

Oh shit. I wasn't giving him any ideas. "Um… I don't think I should say."

He chuckled. "Later, I might make you. Or I could just come up with something else for you now. I don't want you to be disappointed."

"No!"

He glared at me.

"I mean, only if that's what you want, Daddy." I originally meant the words mockingly, but as they came out, I realized I truly meant them. I wanted to do what Graham asked.

"What I want is for you to put this on and then these." He pulled a pair of bright blue skinny jeans out of his bag. They were the same color as the rope he'd used on me before. "I love this color against your skin," he said, as if responding to my unspoken question.

"Then I'm happy to wear it for you." I took the pants and the jockstrap. "Do I get a shirt, Daddy?"

"You do." He pulled out a cropped t-shirt with a mermaid on it. "If this is too much, you can always say no."

I snatched it from him and held it against me. "No way. I love this."

He gave me the smile that meant he was pleased with me. I loved that smile.

"Where are we going for dinner? Can you tell me now?"

"Casa Lucas."

My mouth dropped open. You had to get reservations for Friday nights months in advance. "How?"

"Allen plays soccer with the owner."

"Oh, yeah. I remember something about him being on a rec league soccer team and wondering how many of his teammates knew what else he did."

Graham smiled. "That would be interesting to find out."

I stripped quickly and pulled on the jockstrap and then the jeans, which fit like they'd been made for me. "How did you know my size?"

He studied something on the ceiling. "I may or may not have stolen your red ones."

"So that's where they were. I thought Sean took them."

He laughed. "No, it was me, but I have them to give back."

I ran my hands over my ass, turning to admire myself from different angles. "You're forgiven, because these are amazing."

"Shirt too," he insisted. I pulled it on, smoothed it down, and wow I looked really good, which was confirmed when I heard Graham suck in his breath.

"Damn, boy. Now I just want to get you right back out of those."

I rubbed my cock, which was responding to his appreciative stare. "I would do anything to please you, Daddy. If you need a taste of me first—"

"Brat!" He slapped my ass. "Even if I did take a taste, you wouldn't get to come."

"I need you, Daddy."

"I know, boy, but you're going to wait."

"Yes, sir." I knew arguing wouldn't do me any good.

"I've missed you so much." Graham squeezed me tight.

"I missed you too." I kissed his neck, and he turned his head and took possession of my lips. His warm tongue pushed into me, and I opened for him, tilting my head back and letting him fuck my mouth.

When I sucked on his tongue, he groaned, the sound vibrating through me and making my dick ache.

"These pants are too tight for me to get this hard," I said when he pulled back.

"Then you'll have to control yourself until I'm ready for you to take them off."

I whined, but his stern look silenced me. How did he manage to look so serious and so fucking hot all at once?

"Will you be comfortable with me calling you boy at dinner tonight? Or do you want to hold back on the role play with Leo there?"

I considered that. If we were going to play at the club and Leo already knew, then I shouldn't be too embarrassed, and yet, just the thought of it made my face heat. Was it a sexy embarrassed, though? I couldn't decide. "I don't know."

He studied me for a moment. "Does that mean you want me to decide?"

Did it? It would be so much easier to let him choose. "Yes."

"Then you'll be my boy all night."

As soon as he said it, I knew it was what I wanted too. "Thank you, Daddy."

"You're welcome. Now come on. You need to do your makeup before we go out, and I don't want us to be late."

"Did you pick out makeup for me too, Daddy?"

"Nothing new this time; I want you to wear the pink lipstick you wore at the wedding. Other than that, you can surprise me."

"Do you want to watch me put it on?"

"I do, but I have to get dressed."

"I'll save the lipstick for last then. I know how you love watching that part."

He cupped my cheek. "You're the best boy ever."

I started for the bathroom and then turned back. "What about shoes? I have my short black boots with me."

He smiled. "Those are perfect."

"Daddy, you didn't have to bring me all these presents. I don't want you to spend too much on me."

"I wanted to buy these things for you, and it isn't a hardship for me."

I considered whether to protest further. They weren't outrageous gifts. The jeans were pricey ones, but I wouldn't think much of buying him something comparable, so I decided my conscience could handle it.

"Thank you, Daddy."

"You're welcome. Now go. If you make us late, I'll have to come up with an especially wicked punishment."

I bit my lip, like I was considering whether that might be exactly what I wanted. But then I smiled. "I'll be good, Daddy. Because that's what you like."

"I do. Makeup now."

I scurried into the bathroom.

***

When we stepped into Casa Lucas, Graham put his arm around me and pulled me to him. I could feel protective vibes coming off him. Then I noticed I was getting a number of appreciative looks from both men and women.

"You know exactly how to dress me up, Daddy."

"I do, boy. And I love that everyone is looking."

"You also love that I'm yours."

He chuckled. "Yes, that too."

I put my arm around his waist and squeezed him tight. "So do I."

A broad-shouldered man with dark hair waved to us from a corner booth. Graham waved back, and we headed in his direction.

"You beat us here," Graham said. "I'm impressed."

Leo sniffed. "You think I'm always late, because you're insanely punctual."

"Says the man who's nearly made us miss our plane every time we've traveled together."

"No one should be required to arrive hours early just to take a flight. It's nonsense."

Graham turned to me. "Avery, this is Leo. For some strange reason, he's my best friend."

Leo held out his hand. When we shook, his grip was firm but not crushing. I couldn't help noticing his hand was even bigger than Graham's. He was stocky, with dark hair and eyes, and he had a presence that left no question he was in charge. That must come in handy if there was any trouble at his club. It was also hot as hell.

I realized I was staring and glanced over at Graham.

"He's hot. He knows it. You might as well go ahead and stare."

Leo snorted. "The two of you were watched by nearly everyone in here as you walked in. You look amazing together. And you were right about that shirt." Leo winked at me, and heat rose to my face.

"Did you help him pick it out?" I asked.

"Help isn't exactly the right word," Graham said. "He heckled me as I picked out things for you."

"Someone has to make sure he does things right." Leo inclined his head toward me, like he was pretending to ignore Graham's presence. "He's crazy about you. So I'm trying to make sure he doesn't screw this up."

I grinned at him. "Thank you."

The server came to our table then. "Do you know what you'd like to drink, gentlemen?"

"I'll have a margarita on the rocks," Leo said.

Graham nodded. "Same for me."

I considered joining in, but tequila always hit me fast and hard, and I needed a clear head for playing later. "I'll have a glass of the red sangria."

Our server smiled. "Of course. I'll be right back with those. Be sure to check out our specials, which are on the menu insert. I highly recommend the ceviche sampler as an appetizer. Tonight's varieties are grouper, a mix of shrimp and octopus, and smoked tuna, which is my favorite."

My mouth nearly fell open. "That sounds amazing."

"Go ahead and bring us one of those," Graham said.

I smiled at him as she headed toward the kitchen. "Thank you."

"You're welcome, boy. I love seeing you smile like that."

Leo frowned. "Your devotion is even more intense in person."

Graham glared at him.

"Does he really talk about me that much?" I asked, unable to help myself.

"Yes, and he goes all mushy just like that." He waved a hand in Graham's direction. "I take it he's treating you right?"

"Yes, sir. Very much so." Heat rushed to my face. The "sir" just slipped out. Leo was so obviously a Dom, I couldn't help it.

"Hmm." He glanced at Graham. "Manners too. I think he is a keeper."

"Leo." Graham's voice held a warning quality.

Leo grinned, obviously loving how he was getting to his friend. "Graham told me you're a makeup artist."

"I am."

"Well, you certainly look amazing, so I know you have excellent taste."

"Oh, thank you." I glanced at Graham to see if he minded Leo's compliment, but he was looking back and forth between us and smiling. "I love helping people get the look they want or showing them how to use products that flatter them and give them more confidence."

"He's making some of his own products too," Graham said, a huge smile on his face.

Leo's eyes widened. "That's impressive."

"I'd love to have my own makeup line one day. I can't take on that kind of debt right now, but I'm saving toward it."

A look passed between Leo and Graham that I couldn't quite read. Then Leo said, "I have a feeling it will work out."

Just as I was thinking it was time to change the subject, our server returned with our drinks. "Your ceviche will be out shortly. Do you know what entrees you'd like?"

Graham ordered fish tacos, and Leo and I both chose octopus enchiladas.

"That sounds lovely. I'll put your order right in."

"Do you have any questions about Thrust?" I asked before Leo could say more about my business aspirations. I didn't know why I was so reluctant to talk about it. Maybe I thought I'd jinx it somehow if I told too much about my plans.

"I think I'll have more after we go tonight, but I met Allen today. He seems like a great guy."

"He is. I don't know him well, but I do know he is a respected Dom, and he doesn't put up with any shit. He lets tourists in, but they aren't allowed to use the private rooms, and he's not afraid to kick someone out if they're disrespectful in any way."

Graham nodded. "That sounds just like how Leo runs Succumb."

"We haven't had a lot of trouble, fortunately, but I have a very low tolerance for bullshit, so maybe it's just that I scare off the assholes before they really become a problem."

Our server brought the ceviche sampler, and it was every bit as good as she'd said. All conversation stopped as we savored it.

"Wow," Graham said, when we'd polished off every morsel. "I'm thinking about ordering another one."

"Mmm. I wouldn't say no to that," I said. "It was all good, but the smoked tuna was incredible."

Leo licked his lips. "Do you think they'd kick me out if I drank the juice in the bottom of the dish?"

I laughed, and Graham said, "I bet you wouldn't be the first."

As tempting as picking up the bowl was, Leo decided he was more dignified than that. We talked a bit more about the club, and then our entrees came.

I'd just picked up my fork when Leo said, "I've known Graham for eight years, and I don't think I've ever seen him this happy."

His words made Graham blush, and I had to fight the urge to reach up and touch his heated cheek.

"You're good for him. I thought that already from the way he talks about you, but now that I've seen you together, I'm sure of it."

"So I have your blessing?" I asked.

"Boy, you don't need his blessing," Graham said. "You only need mine."

"Oooh." Leo grinned. "I really do like this thing you have going."

Graham growled at him, and we kept the conversation light for the rest of dinner. I described some of the best hiking trails in the area when Leo mentioned he wanted to explore some the next day. I found out Graham and Leo had season tickets for the Broadway Lights series in Charlotte, and Graham promised to get an extra ticket for me for some of the upcoming shows. I told them more about the salon where I worked. Leo said he might come by the next day and try it out since he was due for a haircut anyway.

Graham and Leo argued over who would pay the bill. Ultimately Graham won, but only because Leo backed down. I was a little embarrassed by how hot it made me to see them try to out Dom each other. It was all I could do not to kneel to them both.

"Do you need anything else?" Graham asked, startling me from my thoughts of what he and Leo would be like topping together.

"No, but I'd like to use the restroom. I'm sure it's cleaner than the one at Thrust."

"It's nearly impossible to keep club bathrooms clean." Leo made a face. "It's like a total jizz fest in there even when we have play rooms not that far from the dance floor."

Graham snorted. "As if you haven't—"

"I have a private office and my choice of a number of comfy private rooms."

"Not now, but when you were younger."

"I was an idiot then. And a lot of idiots come into my club."

I couldn't help but laugh. I'd been an idiot more times than I should.

Graham leaned in close and whispered in my ear. "Go on, boy, but be quick. I'm eager to get you on your knees so everyone can see just how good you can be."

I shivered. "Yes, Daddy."

CHAPTER NINE

AVERY

Sean met us in the parking lot, and we all walked into Thrust together. I was surprised how different it felt with Graham right behind me, a hand low on my spine, guiding me. I'd never come here with anyone I planned to play with. I'd either arranged to meet a partner here or arrived hoping to find someone who was interested in the same games I was. This time, I knew exactly what was going to happen, and I was half hard before we got in the door.

Graham had stroked my leg during dinner, skimming his fingers along the edge of my groin, never touching my cock, but coming so close. I could feel the straps of the pink jock pressing into my ass. Graham would love displaying me in it.

"We're going to walk around with Leo for a bit," Graham whispered. "And then Allen has a place reserved for us."

"He does?"

"With a spanking bench."

I shivered.

"I'm not going to cuff you to it, though. You're going to hold yourself in place, and everyone will see how good you are, how much you want to please your daddy."

Now I was all the way hard. I didn't think it would take more than a few strokes to get me off. "Yes, Daddy. I want to make you happy."

"I know you do. You're so good." His warm breath against my ear made me shudder, and his soft tone warmed me all over. He was exactly what I needed.

We walked around the edge of the dance floor, which was crowded and rowdy. When Sean and I came together, we usually ended up right in the middle of those writhing bodies, rubbing up against someone, looking for a good time.

I turned to Sean. "You can go dance if you want to. You don't have to stick with us."

"No, I like this. There's a nice view."

We were standing behind Leo and Graham, and he eyed their asses like they were works of art and he had to memorize every detail.

I rolled my eyes, but I couldn't disagree. Sean had been flirting with Leo as we walked around. But I didn't think Leo was interested or that he was right for Sean. I had a feeling Leo liked men who knelt at the snap of a finger and obeyed his every command. I also had the sense he played a hell of a lot harder than Sean did. Graham had mentioned that Leo trained other Doms in edge play.

I couldn't see Sean agreeing to anything edgy. He preferred spankings that were more about play than pain. Then he wanted to get fucked and walk away. Except for whatever had happened with this mystery man he still wouldn't talk about.

Graham turned and took my arm. "Let's go see some of the play areas."

"You want to come?" I asked Sean.

"Hell, yes." He moved in between Graham and Leo so he could walk by Leo's side. I wanted to warn him he was in way over his head, but he was a grownup, and he could figure that out on his own. I doubted Leo intended to play with anyone tonight, even if he was into Sean, since he was there to decide if he wanted to put in an offer on the club. At least I knew he was a decent guy who would let an overeager Sean down nicely. He probably had men following him around like puppies constantly at Succumb, so I assumed he was used to it.

We stepped into the loudest of the play areas. This area was for scenes that didn't require a lot of concentration, and most people playing here enjoyed being watched. Many were deliberately putting on a show. This was where I usually played. I glanced around at the people who were watching and listened to the sounds of crops and paddles hitting flesh, the grunts and cries they elicited. I saw a man who had three men taking turns fucking him while his Dom petted him, stroking his hair, and encouraging him to lay his head in the Dom's lap.

"This is where we'll be later," Graham murmured, flicking his tongue along the outer edge of my ear. "I want a lot of people to see my boy."

I turned and looked up at him. "I want that too, Daddy."

Leo motioned to us to indicate he was going into the next area, a quieter space for more serious play. Graham took my hand, and we followed him.

We watched a woman tying her sub into a suspension harness and then Graham turned me so I could see a man in a sex swing who was being fisted.

"If you're a good boy, we can do that soon."

"Daddy, I…" My mouth opened and closed, but I couldn't say anything else.

"My boy can take it," Graham whispered.

I wanted to. God, just the thought of Graham's whole hand inside me made my cock jump, but the man I was watching looked like he was in agony. His ass seemed impossibly stretched like something a real body couldn't do. I'd seen men fisted before, but now that I was actually thinking about letting someone do it to me, it seemed terrifying. I'd fantasized about it for years, but I never thought I'd trust a partner enough to allow it.

Could my ass actually open like that?

"I know it looks scary," Graham said. "But we'll go so slow. I'll make sure you love it as much as you want to."

"Daddy." That was all I could manage to say.

The Dom had part of his arm in his sub, and he was slowly moving in and out. His sub whimpered and cried out, but he was hard now, and he looked like he was starting to enjoy it, even shifting his hips to take more. Maybe I could do it. Maybe it would be as good as my fantasies.

We walked away from the men we'd been watching, and I almost ran into Sean when he stumbled. Leo caught his arm to keep him from falling.

"Are you all right?" Leo asked.

I could tell he had the same natural caregiving sense Graham did, and I wished he had a boy of his own. What was wrong with me? I'd been with Graham a few weeks, and I was already turning into a matchmaker.

Sean didn't answer Leo. Instead, he just looked toward the doorway that led into the next room.

A gorgeous, dark-haired man stood there. He was wearing leather pants, a tight black t-shirt, and a dungeon monitor armband. He stepped forward and held out a hand to Leo. From the way he towered over all of us, he had to be at least six four.

"I'm Blake. Allen told me you'd be here tonight. He hired me to handle security a few months ago, so he thought you might want to talk to me. I'm monitoring this room tonight, but I'm about to take a break, so we can go some place quieter if you'd like."

Leo nodded. "That sounds great."

Blake turned to Sean. "How've you been?"

Sean didn't answer. He'd gone pale, and he started to move away slowly.

"Sean?" I called.

"I… I need to go. I have to…"

"I'll be back," I told Graham as I took Sean's arm and led him from the room. "Is that him? The man you were going out with."

Sean's Adam's apple moved up and down as he swallowed. "I… um… Yes."

"Are you sure he didn't hurt you?" Sean looked terrified. I'd never seen him like this before.

"No. It was the other way around."

"You hurt him?"

Sean nodded. "I need to go. I shouldn't have come. I should've known he'd be here. I…"

Graham was walking our way, looking concerned.

"Did you drive here?" I asked.

"No, I took an Uber."

"Come on," Graham said. "We'll walk you out and get you a ride home."

"You don't have to—"

"We're walking you out," Graham said again, and Sean didn't protest anymore. But when we stepped into the bar area, Leo and Blake were right there in a booth.

Blake stood up. "Sean?"

Sean gripped my hand so hard, I thought he might break something.

"Do you have a minute to talk?" Blake's voice was neutral, but I could tell he was on edge.

"I… I don't…"

"Talk to him," Leo said.

I glanced at him, and he mouthed, "Trust me."

"You might feel better if you do," I whispered. "I've never seen you sadder than the day you ended things with him."

Blake held out his hand. I could see Sean's hand shaking as he took it and let Blake pull him close. There was no sign of the bratty, sassy Sean who usually came out to play at Thrust as Sean let himself be led across the room.

I looked back at Leo. "You really think this will be okay?"

He nodded. "I know Blake by reputation, and while he didn't give me any details about what happened with Sean, he said he wants to see if they can work things out."

I let out a long breath. "When Blake broke things off, it messed Sean up. He was a wreck for days after they ended things. I've never seen him like that."

"And you don't know what happened?" Graham asked.

I shook my head. "I'll need to check on him later."

He nodded. "Of course."

Leo glanced toward where Blake and Sean had disappeared. "He needs to take Sean in hand and teach him some discipline."

"Yeah, pretty much." I loved that Leo had figured that out after knowing Sean less than an hour.

"Will he be all right?" Graham asked, looking at me.

"I think so."

Leo nodded. "Allen told me about Blake. He said he's a good man, a former SEAL, and—"

"Hot as fuck," Graham added.

Leo chuckled. "That too."

I scowled at Graham in mock annoyance.

"Do you have something to say, boy?"

I shook my head, unable to keep from laughing. "Just that you're absolutely right."

Graham raised his brows. "I think it's time for us to find our spot."

"Eager to redden my ass?"

"Boy, you're going to get yourself in trouble."

"Sorry, Daddy."

Graham looked at Leo but he waved us away.

"Go on and play. Just text me if you decide to leave."

"We will."

Graham brought me to an area that was roped off. We'd passed it earlier, but it hadn't registered that it might be ours.

He took the rope down and moved the spanking bench around until it was parallel to the back portion of the play area. "I want people to be able to see your red ass and your beautiful pink lips."

"Daddy, I don't know if I can look at people as they watch me."

He cupped my face, bracketing me so I only saw him. "You can close your eyes, boy. You don't have to look, but I want them to see you, to see how you hold yourself, how well you take what I give."

I could see how much he cared for me, but I also saw the flare of lust in his eyes. He loved this, and I wanted to give it to him. "Yes, Daddy. I can do that because it's what you want."

"That's my boy. Now raise your arms."

I did, and he took the hem of my shirt and lifted it up and over my head. He laid it on top of a bag I hadn't seen him bring in. I recognized it though.

"How…?"

"Leo brought it for me earlier."

"I love that you planned all this."

Graham kissed me gently. "That's what a Daddy does. He makes sure everything will be all set for his boy."

I smiled at him, already starting to feel that sense of being somewhere out of time I got when I truly surrendered to him. I loved giving up control to him, especially now that it felt more… real?

That word kept coming up, but it unnerved me. What did it mean that this was my reality, that as Graham's boy I was more me than I'd been before? I hadn't been unhappy or dissatisfied, not seriously. I just hadn't been cared for like I'd longed to be. I'd enjoyed sex. Most of the partners I'd been with were a lot of fun, but with Graham I felt a level of soul-deep satisfaction that was like nothing I'd experienced.

He unzipped my pants and pushed them over my hips. I heard someone whistle as he pushed my pants down. "Keep your eyes on me," Graham said.

I did, and his presence grounded me. When I'd done this before it had been about showing myself off. I was comfortable with my body. I knew I looked good. But tonight my focus was on pleasing Graham. He wanted the people there to see me, so I would let him display me. I wanted to show him how much I appreciated him taking care of me.

Once he had me stripped down to the jockstrap he'd bought me, the one that went so well with my lipstick, he reached into his bag once more. "I have one more surprise for you."

He was holding a pair of pink stilettos. "Will you wear these while I spank you?"

They'd look perfect with the jockstrap. I'd make such a good display for my daddy. "Yes."

He helped me slip them on and then held my hands, making sure I had my balance. "You look amazing in those, boy. I'm going to have to put you in heels more often."

"I'd like that, Daddy. I want to please you."

"I know you do, boy." He rested his hands on my shoulders. "I'm going to spank you and then I'm going to use the crop. Not because you've been bad, but because I want everyone here to see how you can take what I give you, how you can stay on the bench and offer your ass to me, hurt for me."

"Yes, Daddy."

"What's your safeword?"

"Red."

"Will you use it no matter what?"

"Yes, Daddy."

"Nothing matters more to me than you being safe and comfortable, not what I want, not what anyone gets to see. This scene is just a game. Maybe this Daddy dynamic between us isn't anymore, but this, the spanking, me displaying you here, that is a game we can end any time."

I bit my lip. I knew in my head that he wouldn't be angry if I couldn't do this for him, but sometimes it was hard to accept anything other than perfection from myself.

"Boy?"

"Yes, Daddy. You want me taken care of more than anything else."

"That's right." He stroked down my arms. "Yes. I already know what a good boy you are. I already know you can take this, but some days we can't do what we could on others. And sometimes what we think will be a great experience isn't."

"I can do this, Daddy."

He nodded. "You can, but you don't have to."

"I want to."

"Good." He kissed me softly. "I'm going to put a ring on you now to help you. If we were at home, I would expect you to hold back on your own, but this is different."

"Thank you, Daddy."

"I don't want you to come, because your release is mine. It's not for anyone here. I want them to see your obedience, your beautiful reddened ass, but when you come, it's for me."

His words made me dizzy with need for him. I swayed toward him, teetering on the heels, and he squeezed my biceps to hold me up.

"So beautiful," he whispered. Then he reached into his pocket and pulled out a cock ring. He slipped his hand into the pouch of the jock and quickly and efficiently fitted it on me.

I stayed still, even though I desperately wanted to push into his hand.

"Position yourself on the bench."

When he stepped away from me, I shivered. This did not feel like anything I'd done before. I knew there must be people watching, even if they were only seeing us in passing. But I really wasn't aware of them. I was only aware of Graham and the thrum of my own body. I wanted him. I wanted all of this, but it was more than lust. It was a physical need to surrender to him, to please him, one stronger than I'd ever felt before. The world around us seemed muted like when you're on stage for a play and the lights shine in your face. It's so bright you can't really see the audience so you just act as though the stage is the only place in the world. It was like that, except my cock was hard and needy, and I knew it would be a long time before Daddy let me come.

I concentrated on each step, wanting Graham to be proud of how I walked in heels. When I reached the bench, I draped myself over it, gripping the handles at the base and fitting my legs along the padded sides. I saw the cuffs that could be used to hold my wrists and ankles. If I asked him to, Daddy would strap me in and force me to stay there. But that's not what he wanted. And I didn't need it. I only needed him wanting me here.

"Are you comfortable?" Graham asked.

"Yes, Daddy."

"Isn't he beautiful?" Graham asked. "Those pink straps? Those sexy shoes?"

I knew he was speaking to those who were watching. I opened my eyes for a moment to see a crowd of people around us, more than I expected.

"Close your eyes, boy."

Graham placed a blindfold over my eyes so I didn't have a choice about looking. Of course I actually did. I could take the blindfold off, but I wouldn't.

"My boy is so good. He can hold still for his spanking without cuffs, right boy?"

"Y-yes, Daddy." My voice sounded scratchy.

Graham ran his hands over me. "His ass looks so gorgeous when it's all red." He leaned down and I could feel his breath against my ear. "I'm going to start now, boy. I expect you to stay still. You can make as much noise as you want, but you may not come."

"Yes, Daddy." I tried to project my voice so everyone who was watching could hear.

I wasn't sure how well I managed it, but it didn't matter, because Graham slapped my ass and pain exploded over my skin. Breathe, I told myself. Just breathe and relax.

But as the slaps kept coming I tensed, which made them hurt so much more.

"Take a breath, boy," Graham said.

I did, a slow inhale and a long exhale.

"I want to hear you, boy, I want to hear how much it hurts."

"Yes, Da—"

Crack!

His hand came down on me harder than before, and he didn't slow down, spanking me over and over. I whined and whimpered at first, but then I couldn't hold in shouts and cries. I begged him to stop. I wanted to writhe against the bench. I wanted to get up and walk away, but I wasn't going to, because Daddy wanted me there. He wanted everyone to see me.

He slowed down, and I managed to breathe again.

"Beautiful boy, you're so good. You're taking all of this."

"Daddy!" I yelled when he spanked me hard on the sorest part of my ass.

"So good." He rubbed my back. "Just breathe and relax. Your ass is so lovely, all red and hot."

He ran his hands over it, and I shuddered.

"Thank you, Daddy," I said, or at least I thought the words came out. I wasn't completely sure. Everything seemed far away, the pain, the people I knew were watching. Everything but the throb in my cock and the need for Graham to stay with me.

As if he knew what I was thinking, he knelt and laid a hand on the back of my neck. As he spoke, he kept his voice low so no one else could hear. "I'm right here. I'm just giving you a break. I'm going to use a crop on you next."

"Oh, Daddy."

"Is that okay?"

"Yes, please. I want that, Daddy." I loved the sting of the crop, and somehow I knew it would anchor me, bring me back to earth and keep me there. And that would be good, because I was feeling a bit out of control.

"You're so good. Of course I'll give you what you want." He stood and positioned himself behind me. "Exhale."

I did, sinking into the bench.

The crop came down then, slashing over my ass. I cried out. It hurt so bad, worse than I'd remembered.

"Daddy!"

He hit me again.

"You can move, boy, any way you need to as long as your knees stay on the pads and you grip the handholds. Can you do that?"

"Yes, Daddy."

He cracked the crop against me, and I writhed and shook. The next blows came quick, one after another. I thought I screamed at some point, but I wasn't sure. The pain was now a constant throbbing thing. I needed to get away from it, but I also needed to lean into it, to beg for more. I pushed my ass toward the blows, and my body hummed like it was electrified.

"Daddy! Please!" I wasn't even sure what I was begging for.

"Take a slow breath."

I tried, but it took a while before I could. On the exhale he brought the crop down for a final flurry of blows.

After the last one, I sobbed, in agony but also in pleasure, because I'd done everything he wanted.

CHAPTER TEN

GRAHAM

I let out a shuddering breath. I'd known Avery would be beautiful like this, but seeing him straining toward the crop with those pink straps around his ass, his full pink lips and those fuck-me shoes was glorious. He was glorious. And I was so lucky to have his trust.

I slid my hand up and down his back. "You're so good, boy. Everyone loved watching you submit. Thank you for giving me this."

"You're welcome, Daddy." His words were soft, and the way he smiled at me made my chest ache.

"Are you ready for me to take the blindfold off?"

"I... I need."

I knelt beside him and slid my fingers into his hair. "I'm right here. I'm not going to leave you."

"Give me a... few more... minutes."

I stroked his head and just stayed with him until he whispered, "I'm ready now."

He blinked and squinted when I removed the blindfold, and I sat by him until he'd had a chance to adjust to seeing again.

"I'm going to help you up now, okay?"

"Can you take my shoes off first, Daddy? I don't think I can walk in them now."

"Of course, boy." As I removed the heels, he smiled at me looking totally blissed out. I loved that I could do that for him. "How do you feel?"

"Good, but…"

"What is it, baby?"

"I need you to fuck me. Please."

I kissed him softly. "I'll take care of you, boy. We just need to go somewhere private."

He shifted position and winced. I could imagine how much his ass hurt, even sitting on a padded bench. "I'm going to take you to a room and tend your ass, okay?"

He frowned then. "Leo's watching us."

I turned and saw him. He looked away before our eyes met, but not before I saw the longing in his expression, like he wanted the closeness Avery and I had found. It made me ache for him.

I handed Avery a bottle of water and helped him stand. "Can you walk or do you need me to carry you?"

"I think I can walk, Daddy."

He stumbled a bit, and I took his arm. "I won't risk you falling. I'm going to put you over my shoulder and take you to a room where I will fuck you so hard you'll see stars when you come. Then I'll take care of your ass and take you home to bed."

"Yes, Daddy."

I hoisted Avery over my shoulder, careful not to lay my hand across his tender ass. Once we were inside the private room I'd reserved, I laid him on his side on the bed.

"You really were amazing out there. Tell me how you want this."

"On my back."

I sucked in my breath. "That will hurt when your ass rubs on the mattress."

"I need to see you."

"You can ride me if you want."

"Really?"

"This is your reward; you get to choose."

"Daddy, you're so good to me."

I smiled at him. "You really went deep. Are you sure you're okay?"

He nodded. "I… yeah. It felt so good, Daddy."

"All right. Let me get the lube from my bag."

"Okay, Daddy."

Once I had what I needed, I stretched out on my back and told Avery to straddle me.

"Good. Now lean forward, I'm going to get you ready." He moaned as I pushed slick fingers into him, and the sound made my cock jump. "That's right, boy. Open up for me."

He pushed back into me. "More, Daddy."

I worked my fingers deeper, opening them to stretch him more. Then I pulled them free and took hold of his hips. "Take my cock into you slowly."

He reached for me, aiming me toward his hole. I bit my lip as his heat and tightness brought me much too close. I squeezed the base of my dick as he eased his way down, finally having to let go so he could take all of me. "So good, boy. You're fucking perfect."

"Want to ride you, Daddy."

"I know. Take it slow at first, and tell me if it hurts too much."

He shook his head. "Feels so good. Won't last long."

"You don't have to. You can come whenever you're ready."

"Thank you, Daddy."

He lifted off me and sank back down. After a few strokes, he started moving faster. I pulled him down so I could kiss him, and his movements became erratic before he cried out, "I'm coming, Daddy!"

His seed splashed against my chest, and I fought the urge to let go and fill his ass.

"Raise up off my cock," I told him once his breathing slowed a little.

He looked confused. "Daddy, you haven't—"

"Shhh. Just do what I said."

He did, slowly lifting himself until my cock came free. "Now scoop up your cum and rub it on my cock, so I can fuck it back into you."

"Oh, my God, Daddy."

"Do it," I demanded.

He ran his fingers over my chest, gathering up most of his cum. Then he stroked my cock, smearing it around. "This is so dirty, Daddy."

"Fuck yes, it is." It was slick and warm, and my cock jerked in his hand because I was so fucking close, but I wanted to be inside him when I came.

His head dropped back as he lowered himself. My cock eased back into him. I saw he was half hard. Could I hold off enough to make him come again? I hoped so.

"Jerk yourself off, boy."

His hand slid across my chest. "Can I use my cum too, Daddy?"

I almost lost it then. "God, yes!"

He rubbed his hand over my sticky chest and then started working his cock. I held his hips and drove up into him, hard and deep. "You're going to come again for Daddy, aren't you? You're going to come thinking about me fucking you with my dick coated in your spunk. You're going to be so full when I shoot in your ass."

"So sore, Daddy, not sure I can." He groaned, the sound low and anguished.

I took hold of his hips, tilting them forward, giving me a better angle. "I want you to come again. I know you can."

"Daddy!" he cried as I hit his sweet spot.

"Yes, boy, feels good, doesn't it?"

"So good, Daddy. Please, give me more."

"Yes, baby, I'm going to fuck you so hard." I used my grip on his hips to move him up and down as I thrust.

"Daddy. I'm close. You... you're going to make me come. I didn't think—"

I squeezed his ass then, right where it was bright red. He cried out, his ass squeezing my cock so tightly, I was coming before he'd finished.

"So hot," he said as he collapsed against my chest.

I dropped back onto the mattress, trying desperately to catch my breath.

"I feel it, Daddy," he said, fighting to get the words out around ragged breaths.

"What, boy?"

"Your cum leaking from my ass."

I put my hand down, wanting to feel it too. "Mmm. I love filling you with cum."

He sighed against me, and I loved how content he sounded. I let him catch his breath for a few moments, then I kissed the top of his head. "I'm so proud of you. You did so good out there and looked so hot. I know you want to sleep, but I need to get you home, and I have to check in with Leo. You should make sure Sean's okay too."

After I'd gotten us cleaned up and put arnica on Avery's ass, I let Leo know I was taking Avery home. Sean assured Avery he was fine and said he'd text tomorrow. My boy was so exhausted when I got him home, I doubted he'd remember me putting him to bed.

When I slipped under the covers, I pulled him against me and held him tight. I was in awe of how thoroughly he'd given himself to me. Every time we were together, I became more and more convinced that I didn't ever want to let him go.

CHAPTER ELEVEN

GRAHAM

While Avery was at work the next day, I went shopping for the ingredients to make Steak Diane, which I remembered him loving when we went out to dinner our first weekend together at Misty Mountain Lodge. I also got some freshly harvested fingerling potatoes and ingredients for a Caesar salad. Avery had to work later than usual for a Saturday because of a bridal party, so I intended to have dinner ready just after he arrived home. I would fill him full of good food before I told him my proposal for funding his makeup line.

I was still nervous he would balk at me giving him the capital he needed, but I hoped that he would accept the idea of paying me back slowly once the business was profitable. He deserved a chance, I believed in him, and I had the money. Why wouldn't I use it to help him with this dream? I tried not to let myself worry about his reaction as I worked in the kitchen, but I failed miserably. By the time Avery called saying he was nearly done at the salon, I was a mess. I poured myself a glass of whiskey, hoping it would take the edge off my nerves. I polished it off quickly, but I still felt like I might come out of my skin. I wanted another, but I needed to be sober to talk to Avery, so I resisted the temptation.

He arrived a few minutes later, and after a long, lingering kiss, I motioned toward the balcony. "Have a seat, pour yourself a glass of wine, and I'll bring dinner out."

"Oh wow. Is that Steak Diane?"

"It is. Now do what I said."

"Yes, Daddy. Thank you."

"You deserve it, boy. You've had a long day after a long night."

"I liked my long night better, though I'm pleased with how the wedding party looked."

"I'm sure you worked magic like you always do."

Avery loved the dinner as much as I'd hoped, and while we ate, he told me about his day and the bride who was so nervous she started crying while he was doing her makeup.

"I had to start over, but I think she looked even better the second time."

I smiled. I'd hardly eaten anything, because I was too busy watching him. "You're amazing."

"It's just makeup."

"Not just your makeup skills, everything about you."

His cheeks went pink, and I reached for his hand. "I want to ask you something, and I need you to promise to hear me out before you say yes or no."

He frowned. "You're making me nervous."

Rather than apologizing or trying to reassure him, I just dove in. "I want to invest in your makeup line."

"Invest?"

"I want to be your backer, so you can start your business now."

Avery shook his head. "I won't take money from you."

"I asked you to hear me out before you responded."

He took a deep breath. "I can't do this as role play."

I fought back annoyance. "I wasn't... That wasn't a command as your daddy. That's what I would ask of anyone I was making a business proposition to."

"Oh." He looked away. "I'm sorry."

I laid my hand over his. "It's not your fault. Neither of us are used to this or understand exactly where our lines are. You were right to stop me and be clear about what you needed. I just really want to help you. Please consider my offer."

He nodded. "Okay, but what if I never make any profit?"

"Then I don't get a return on my investment. It certainly wouldn't be the first time that has happened."

"But you're not just some investment firm. You're... We're... I don't want to complicate this. There's already so much we're unsure of, and you live in Charlotte and have a life there, and I'm here, and I love playing Daddy and boy, but I can't let you support me, but if I'll still have to work then I won't have time to create products to sell, and—"

"Take a breath."

He did, a shaky one. Then he looked away and wiped at his eyes. "I'm sorry. I think all of this has just been building, and... I don't know. I didn't mean to freak out on you. It's really great of you to offer, but I just can't."

I squeezed his hand. "Things have been amazing for these last weeks, but our relationship has been sort of removed from reality." Something I'd been trying to ignore. "We aren't always going to immediately agree on everything. If we're going to keep doing this, we'll argue some, and we'll have to talk things through. Then hopefully have amazing make-up sex."

Avery smiled. "Yeah, and I might need discipline for talking back."

"You just might."

"But, a relationship can't just be weekends of hot fucking, can it?"

My stomach knotted. He wasn't saying we should break up, was he? "Not for the long term maybe, but it's not a bad start. I know we're going to have to consider a lot of things and find a way to work through them, but I'm here for that. I want you, all of what you have to offer, not just your ass."

We sat in silence for several moments. I traced patterns on his palm as my pulse whooshed in my ears. I was afraid of saying something to break this fragile thing between us. Our bond seemed so strong when I had him on his knees or bent over the bed, but right now I didn't feel the certainty about our future that I had the night before. I was scared all the complications of age, distance, and income would defeat us.

"I want you to know that even if we weren't together, if Carter and Felicity had told me about your business plans, I would be willing to loan you money."

"Loan, not give."

"I said you could pay me back once you were making a profit. This is a long-term deal."

"Why would you do that? I mean if we weren't even…"

"Because you're talented, and I have money, and I would do anything for my kids if they asked."

He blew out a long breath. "I need a lot of money."

"Fortunately, that's what I have."

"I'll think about it, all right?"

I pushed my chair back, circled the table, and knelt by him. "Thank you. I want this for you. I want to help you make your dream come true."

He took my hands, then leaned down and kissed me. "I know you do, and that means a lot to me. I just need time to think."

We didn't talk about Avery's business—or any of the other issues hanging over us—for the rest of the weekend. We watched movies and fucked, went for a hike and stopped for a hand job in the woods, went out to brunch and I damn near begged him for a bathroom blowjob. But, though neither of us mentioned it, something felt off. We were less in sync with each other than we'd ever been, and we were stepping back from our role play far more than usual. Not consciously, at least not on my part, but it felt natural because there was more distance between us. Being a daddy felt more like a game, like it had with other boys I'd played with. That scared me, because even the day Avery and I met, we'd fallen into those roles like they were made for us.

When we kissed goodbye, I didn't say anything about how concerned I was, because I was afraid of making things worse. I told Avery I'd come back on Friday, and I told myself things would be better then, and we'd figure this out.

But as I opened the door, I couldn't let myself leave without saying something. I let go of the doorknob and turned to face him. "I could move here.

It wouldn't be that hard. I loved living in Asheville, and I only left because I needed distance from Louise and a place to explore life as a gay man without our old judgmental friends appearing everywhere I went."

Avery shook his head. "But your life is in Charlotte now. Your friends, your work."

"I own plenty of properties in this area too. It just hasn't been my focus lately. I'd have to drive down to Charlotte every few weeks, but I don't have to live there. I can hire someone to manage a lot of the work there. I can have meetings over Skype. There are lots of ways to work this out."

"No, I can't let you move just for me. Not now, not yet."

Those words stung. Did he not feel as strongly about staying together as I did? "But, I—"

"It's too much, too soon."

"Is it really?" I asked.

Avery looked down. "No. Yes. I don't know. What I feel for you seems so strong and that scares me. What if you move and then…"

I didn't even want to think about us breaking up, but he deserved an answer. "Then I'm living in a beautiful town. I can see my children more often, and Leo will be here a lot if he buys Thrust."

"I need to think about this. All of this. You're offering so much. I should be happy, but I… I don't know what to say."

I pulled him into my arms and held him tight. "It's all right not to know. But I couldn't leave without telling you that I would move for you. I would do anything for you. That's how important you are to me."

"Thank you, Daddy."

I kissed him, trying to make him feel how much I cared, since communicating physically came so much easier to us.

A few moments later, he pulled back. "You should go. You said you had an early meeting tomorrow."

"Okay, I'll text you when I'm home."

He closed the door behind me, and it was all I could do not to turn around again. I wanted to scoop him up, carry him to bed, and fuck him until we forgot all the things we were worried about.

CHAPTER TWELVE

AVERY

My phone buzzed as I was watching a movie with Sean on Thursday night. It was Graham.

Do you have time to talk?

Instead of texting back I just motioned to Sean to keep watching without me and called Graham as I headed to my room.

"It's good to hear your voice," I said when he answered.

"It's good to hear you too."

"So what's up?"

"Leo has decided to buy Thrust, and he wants to have dinner tomorrow night to celebrate. I don't want to be late coming to Asheville, especially when I have to leave earlier than usual on Sunday, but—"

"You should go."

"Are you sure?"

"Yes."

"I'll stick to soda so I can drive, and I'll leave early. I bet I can make it to Asheville by eleven."

I didn't want him cutting his evening short for me, but I really wanted to see him, maybe even more than I had any other time. Because despite him saying he was willing to move here, I'd worried he might decide things had become too complicated and not come back at all. I kept wondering when he'd finally decide this couldn't work. At least after hearing his voice I felt better.

"Why don't I come to Charlotte instead? I can be there whenever you think you'll be done, and then we'll have more time together. You shouldn't have to do all the driving."

"Don't you have to work on Saturday?"

"I already decided to take Saturday off. I… um… Other than the wedding, I haven't taken vacation time in forever, and I thought we would need more time because… well, last weekend was…"

"Thank you. I want more time with you too."

"Text me your address, and I'll be there when you get home from Leo's celebration."

"I have a better idea. Why don't you come with me?"

"To dinner?"

"Yes. I'd love to introduce you to Max and Foster, the other guys who will be there."

I stood and paced, even more nervous than I had been.

"Or if you don't want to, I can leave you a key for my house."

"No. I mean, yes, I'll go." We needed to be open to meeting each other's friends, and I liked Leo, so…

"Thank you. You're amazing."

"So are you."

"I've got to go, but I'll send my address, and I'll see you tomorrow."

"I should be able to be there around seven. Will that be okay?"

"Yes. I'll be home, and we can head to Leo's dinner soon after you get here."

I ended the call and went back to the living room. Sean paused the movie when I sat down. "What's up?"

"Nothing. I was just talking to Graham."

He studied me for a moment. "That is not your usual talking to Graham face."

"I'm going to Charlotte this weekend instead of him coming here."

"And that has you worried?"

"I'm not worried." I was so worried I thought I might come apart.

"You're staring at your phone."

"He's texting me his address, and I want to look it up."

Sean frowned. "You don't know where he lives?"

"I know he lives in Charlotte, but I've never been to his house."

"And you never asked him anything about it?"

"No." Was that strange? Whether it was or not, it proved we'd been existing in a bubble.

Sean grinned. "I guess you've been too busy fucking."

"We talk." Graham and I were more than just sex. I knew that much.

"While you recover for the next round?"

I clenched my hands into fists. "Sean!"

"It's normal to be like that when things are all new. Who needs real life when a man like Graham will give you anything you want?"

Graham really would give me anything I wanted, wouldn't he? He'd move here, loan me money to start a business with no guarantee of ever being paid back in full. But I wouldn't let him do any of that, because I was too stubborn.

"I want to talk to you about something," I told Sean. "But you have to be serious. I feel weird talking to Felicity since Graham's her father-in-law, but I need to know you won't laugh at me."

"Are you going to confess to some kinky shit you're doing?"

"I call him Daddy, and he calls me boy, and I totally get off on it. There. That's out of the way."

Sean made a strangled sound. And I kind of loved that I'd thrown him off-balance.

"But that's not what I wanted to say."

Sean's expression turned serious. "In the interest of confessions, I tried pony play with Blake, but he said I didn't have enough discipline. He wants to teach me how to be obedient, and I kind of want him to, but he scares me."

Whoa. Sean was finally talking. "He scares you because he's so dominant?"

Sean shook his head. I waited for him to say more, but he didn't.

"Then why?"

"I feel too much when I'm with him. I want to give him everything he asks for, not just because it's hot, but because I want to please him. I want him to fix the mess I've made of my life, but it's wrong to depend on someone like that."

"Are you sure it's wrong if it's what you both want? Maybe it would be good for you." A few months ago, before meeting Graham, I might not have felt the same way, but after being his boy, I was absolutely sure of what I said.

"I don't know. Don't I just need to man up and be an adult?"

I rolled my eyes. "Like that ever works. Look, you can be a mess, but you're hardly failing at adulting. You pay your rent on time, and even though you keep changing career paths, you take what you're doing seriously. You're a capable adult, despite eating Cocoa Puffs for dinner half the time. That's your choice. Whatever you might do with Blake won't change that."

Sean didn't look convinced. "I asked him if we could just go out casually, do some scenes, enjoy each other, but either we do this his way or not at all."

"So he won't compromise?"

"I can't blame him for that. It's because I hurt him. He told me he wanted to be serious, and I laughed at him and then told him to just get on with it and spank me. He called an end to our scene and after bringing me home, he said he didn't want to see me anymore."

"If you're interested in him, and you do seem to be, then at least think about whether his way could work. And if not, maybe if he sees you're willing to try, you can find a compromise then. You just have to be honest about what you're feeling."

"Listen to you, Mr. Maturity."

"Nothing like sage relationship advice from an expert who's been in one two-month-long relationship with his best friend's father-in-law."

"Exactly."

We both laughed, then he said, "I'm sorry. I totally derailed our conversation with my confession."

"Did it feel good to finally talk about Blake?"

He seemed to consider that for a moment. "Yeah. It did. I was worried you'd be pissed at me for how I treated him."

I shook my head. "I don't expect you to be perfect. If you didn't care that you'd hurt him, if you weren't worried about it, then I'd be mad. But you admitted you fucked up, which shows me you're exactly who I thought you were, even if you pretend to be a heartless asshole sometimes."

Sean huffed. "Only with men who are heartless assholes too."

"Maybe you shouldn't fuck men like that."

He sighed. "The decent guys always want more than I can give."

"There's a difference between can't and won't."

"Maybe, but that's enough about me. Confess something other than your kinky sex shit."

"Pony play is just as kinky as anything I do."

He waved me off. "Whatever."

"Graham offered me money to start my makeup line, however much I need."

"Oh wow. What did you say?"

"That I'd think about it, but I'm uncomfortable just taking money from him."

"Won't you have to pay him back?"

"Only after my business is making money, which might never happen."

"It also might. For all you know, you might become richer than he is."

I snorted. "Little chance of that."

"There's always a chance," Sean said. "You should take the money. You've been wanting to do this forever, and he's offering you the opportunity."

"But I'm indebted to him enough already."

"Why, because he cares for you? That's a gift, and it's one you deserve."

His words knocked the breath out of me. He was right. Graham didn't expect anything from me. "But what if… What if we don't last?"

"I think you will. You've got that totally in love forever thing going."

I stared at him. "We what?"

"Shut up. You so know you do."

I knew what I thought I felt, what I hoped he felt too, but I couldn't talk about it.

"If you did break up, would he expect the money back?"

I shook my head. "He says all investments are a gamble, and this is no different than him buying a property. He never knows how it will turn out."

"Please at least consider it."

"I already told Graham I would."

CHAPTER THIRTEEN

AVERY

Friday night I pulled my ancient Corolla into the driveway of Graham's house, which turned out to be a mansion on a lake. It was made of light gray stone with plenty of windows, gas lanterns at the entrance, and a dark red door. No wonder he wasn't as awed by the Misty Mountain Lodge as I was. His house was probably fancier. I felt so wrong standing at his front door in jeans, a faux retro rainbow shirt, and fuck-me red lipstick. Did I really belong in his world?

Hopefully, after seeing me here, he'd still think I did. I hoisted my bag up on my shoulder and rang the bell. Footsteps approached, and then Graham answered the door wearing a navy pinstriped suit. My mouth dropped open as I forgot everything but how fucking hot he was. I'd thought I remembered how good he'd looked in a tux, how I'd been unable to resist walking over to him when I saw him by the ballroom windows, but my memory had not been doing him justice.

Graham smiled. "Like what you see, boy?"

"Yes, so much."

"Then get in here."

I stepped in, and Graham closed the door behind me.

"Put your bag down and turn around."

I obeyed without thinking, and that felt good, really good, like things were supposed to between us.

I placed my hands on the wall and spread my legs. He stepped behind me and took hold of my hips, pulling them back to let me feel his cock against my ass.

"I've missed you, boy."

"I've missed you too, Daddy."

"I don't even want to wait to get you upstairs. I just want to fuck you right here."

"Please," I whined, fully hard now and ready to beg for him to do exactly what he wanted.

"Don't move."

He walked away, and I tried to take slow breaths to calm my racing heart. I wanted this, wanted him to yank my pants down, pull out his cock, and drive in, no prep, no time to undress, just the need to get his dick in me.

I glanced his way when I heard him return. He was carrying a bottle of lotion that I guessed he'd gotten from the downstairs bathroom. "This is going to have to do for lube, boy."

I nodded. "Fuck me, Daddy. I don't need to go slow."

He reached around me to fondle my cock. "I know what my boy needs. He's a slut for my cock, and he needs it inside him."

"Yes, God yes." How did he have me this crazy this fast?

He leaned down and licked at the edge of my ear, drawing a whine from me. "I want to push right into you, make you take it, give it all to you."

"Yes, Daddy."

"Do you remember your safeword?"

"It's red, Daddy. Please, I want this."

"I know you do." He unfastened my pants and pushed them and my briefs over my ass, letting them pool at my ankles.

"Don't take your hands off the wall. Don't struggle or try to control this. All I want you to do is offer your hole."

"Fuck." How did he know I needed it rough like this? I heard the rustle of fabric and then the slick sound of him greasing his cock up.

He dug his fingers into my ass cheeks and pulled them open. I tensed, expecting it to hurt when he pushed in, but he surprised me by drizzling lotion down my crack.

He smeared it around my entrance with the tip of his cock.

"Brace yourself," he whispered in my ear, his warm breath tickling me.

I pressed all my fingers into the wall and arched my back, presenting my ass to him.

"Good boy, you know what your daddy needs."

He teased me again, brushing my hole with his cock. Then he pressed in, not hard but relentlessly, pushing forward, opening me up. I couldn't help trying to pull away from him. I wanted this badly, but the instinct to fight his invasion was too strong. He slapped my ass.

"Boy, this is my hole, give it to me."

"Yes, Daddy."

He gripped my hips to hold me in place and pushed in harder.

"Fuck, oh fuck."

"Relax and open for me, boy."

"It burns, Daddy."

141

"You can take it, boy." He pulled out, and the sensation was a counter to the pain. But he didn't wait before driving back in harder than before.

I cried out, writhing in his grip.

He pulled out again and caressed my side. "You're a good boy. You can do this for me."

"Yes, Daddy, I'm good. I'll take it. I'll take all of it."

"That's right, you will." He drove in until he was all the way in and his body was pressed against mine.

"That's it. You're so tight, boy. You'd never think I could fit a dildo in there next to my cock."

I whimpered. "That felt so good, Daddy." He reached between us and ran his finger down my crack until he came to the stretched rim of my hole. He pressed against his cock, slipping the tip of his finger inside.

"Fuck. That's… Fuck."

"You could take so much more than this," he said. "You could take my whole hand."

"Yes, Daddy, I want to."

He pulled his finger out and took hold of my hips. "But right now, I just want a simple, hard fuck, and that's what I'm going to have."

"Please."

He drove into me, pushing me against the wall, my face pressed into the cool surface. He didn't slow down as he thrust deep, over and over.

"Don't come," he ordered as I was getting near the edge.

"Daddy, I don't know if I can wait."

"You can!"

"Please," I begged as he kept going, hitting my sweet spot just right, lighting me up with pleasure.

"I love your ass, boy. I love how greedy it is for my cock."

"Yes, Daddy. I love your cock."

"I'm going to come in you, boy, and then if you're good, I'm going to suck you off while my cum drips down your legs."

"Fuck, Daddy. Please. I can't—"

"You better, because it's what I want. I like good little boys."

"I'm good. So good, Daddy."

"Yes. You. Are." He punctuated each word with a thrust. Then he drove in hard and shuddered. "Feel that. Feel me coming in you."

I bit down on my lip and dropped a hand to my cock, squeezing it tight at the base, desperate to hold back my orgasm.

Finally he finished pumping out his release inside me. When he pulled out, I loved the obscene feeling of his cum running out of me and down my legs. "Turn around, boy."

I did, and Graham sank to his knees and took my cock in his mouth. There was no teasing, just efficient sucking. I was ready to come in seconds. He pulled off and worked me with his hand. "Come for me, boy."

I cried out, my release hitting almost instantly. My cum coated Graham's hand, and when I'd finished, he slid his fingers along my thigh, scooping up some of his own cum and then lifting his fingers to my mouth. "Taste us both."

I groaned, my cock never softening as I sucked my cum and his from his fingers. Then he kissed me and I slid my tongue along his, silently asking him to taste us too.

When he pulled back, he glanced down and saw that I was fully hard again, already needing more. "So needy, such a good, slutty boy."

"Thank you, Daddy."

"Thank you for driving here, for taking the day off, for being amazing."

He drew me into his arms, and when I laid my head on his shoulder, it felt just right. Maybe things would be okay after all.

***

I smiled as everyone else laughed at something Leo had just said. I hadn't been listening closely. I was too busy watching Graham smiling at his friends, looking so comfortable here. It wasn't like me to be quiet, even when I was with people I didn't know. I genuinely liked Leo as well as Max, who was Succumb's bookkeeper, and Foster, Leo's assistant manager, but I found myself just listening or watching instead of participating in the conversation.

They weren't intentionally leaving me out, but most of the conversation centered around stories about the club. Some of which were hilarious, like when one of the servers "tripped" and spilled a pitcher of ice water on a Dom who was acting like an asshole to a sub who had no interest in him. The man had slunk out of the club looking like a drowned rat, his hair matted and flattened. Or another where a new-to-the-scene Max had managed to dismantle a sex swing while nervously toying with it as he negotiated with a Dom. That story had a good ending, though. Max and the Dom ended up together for nearly a year.

I knew I shouldn't be jealous of Graham and his friends. Of course they had shared history just like I had with Felicity, Sean, and many of the other stylists at Oasis Asheville. But I couldn't help thinking how Graham had a life here in Charlotte, a good life, that I wasn't part of. The only way I could ever truly be part of it was if one of us moved, and that wasn't fair to either of us.

The server came and asked if we wanted another round.

"Yes," Max said. "It's on me this time."

"None for me," I said. I didn't want to get drunk even though it might help me stop feeling so hurt. If I was hung over in the morning, I wouldn't force the conversation that needed to happen between me and Graham.

Graham scooted closer to me and leaned in to whisper. "Are you all right?"

"Yeah, I've just got a headache, and I'm tired. I didn't sleep well last night." That wasn't a lie. I'd lain awake thinking about seeing Graham again, about how strained things had been the weekend before. "Would you mind if I went on back to your house?"

"I can leave too," Graham said.

"No, I want you to enjoy this. Stay out however long you want, and we'll have all day tomorrow."

"But you drove down here, and—"

"You've already made the trip worthwhile."

Graham grinned, and it made my pulse speed up. He was so gorgeous and caring and good. The thought of not being with him hurt like I was being cut in two, but I needed to do what was right for him. If he was happy here in Charlotte, I couldn't ask him to move.

You didn't ask, he offered.

Graham frowned. "I don't like you leaving on your own."

"I'll take a Lyft. It'll be fine."

He studied me for a moment and then nodded. "All right. But you text me when you get back to my house. Do you have the spare key I gave you?"

"Yes, Daddy." I fought the urge to roll my eyes as I reached into my pocket and held it up. I had asked him to take care of me, and he was trying to do just that.

"Do you two need a room?" Leo asked.

Graham flipped him off as he leaned in to kiss me. Oblivious to the others, I wrapped my arms around his neck and opened for him. When he took possession of my mouth, all my concerns melted.

"Tomorrow I'm going to make sure you remember how to listen to your daddy."

"Please." The word came out in a sexy purr.

"Now go. If you have any trouble or need anything, please call me."

"I will."

I turned to Leo. "Congratulations again. I can't wait to see what you'll do with Thrust."

"If he runs it like he does Succumb, it will be fantastic," Foster said.

I nodded. "I'm sure it will be. It was nice meeting you, Foster, and you too, Max."

"Tell Graham he has to bring you to Succumb sometime," Max said.

I didn't respond to that. I simply said, "Have a good rest of your night. I'm sure I'll see you again sometime."

Graham stood when I did and insisted on walking me to the door. When my Lyft pulled up, he said, "Go home, take some ibuprofen—it's in the center drawer in my bathroom—then go to bed, naked."

"Yes, Daddy." A moment later, the car whisked me away.

***

I woke early the next morning to the warm feeling of Graham spooning me. I wasn't sure when he'd gotten in. I had only a vague memory of him kissing my neck as he snuggled against me. I needed to go to the bathroom, so I carefully lifted his arm and slid out from under it. By the time I emptied my bladder and drank some water, I knew I wasn't likely to fall back asleep. I needed coffee, and while Graham had given me a brief tour of the house the night before, I wanted to explore. Not spy really, just find out what I could learn about him from the things he left out for anyone to see.

I pulled on my sleep pants and headed downstairs. Before going to the kitchen, I checked out the books on the shelf in the living room. There were a lot of biographies, thrillers, mysteries, and a not insignificant collection of Harlequins. The latter made me grin, but I supposed it made sense considering Graham's affection for romcoms—a confession I'd forced out of him our first day together.

He also had a shelf of colored glassware, enough that he must be at least a semi-serious collector. There were vases, bowls, wine glasses, and what I guessed were dessert cups in red, royal blue, and emerald green. The glass was especially beautiful in the early morning sun. He'd situated the shelf in the perfect place to catch the light coming through the French doors that led to the deck. I'd had no idea about his collection or what he liked to read or anywhere near enough about his life when he wasn't with me in Asheville.

I stepped into the next room. I'd thought it would be an office, but it wasn't. A beautiful baby grand piano stood by a bay window, which faced the back yard. Did Graham play? He must. He didn't strike me as the type who would own a piano if he didn't.

I crossed the room, drawn to the well-polished instrument. There were a few books on the stand, one filled with waltzes and the other a collection of country dances. I tried to picture Graham playing the piano, reading a biography in his well-lit living room, and searching antique shops for glassware. None of that seemed wrong, but it also wasn't a side he'd shown me. How well did I know him outside of sex, and how would I ever know much more when we only had weekends and not even all of those?

He'd seemed sincere when he said he was willing to move to Asheville, but after looking at all this and going out with him and his friends, I couldn't understand why he'd want to leave his life here. There were so many things we needed to talk about. It was easy to kiss him and fall into bed—or against the wall or down on my knees. I wanted to do what he said, be what he needed, and it felt so right, but last weekend had shown us we couldn't keep things as they were forever.

I brushed my hand over the piano keys, letting some of the high notes tinkle out over the still room. Then I walked into the kitchen. The coffee pot was on the counter and luckily, Graham stored the coffee and filters in the cabinet right above it.

While the coffee brewed, I stepped onto the back deck. The sun was coming up, but it was far from bright yet, and the air, while not quite cool, was far more refreshing than it would be later. I walked down the steps into the yard. A few terraced gardens led to a gravelly area near the lake. The closest garden had a bed of roses that didn't look too healthy. Some of their leaves were yellowed, and many of them were wilted. As I looked closer, I saw he'd labeled them, and they looked fairly newly planted. When I saw the ones with pale pink and orange variegated blooms, I realized these were some of the varieties he'd shown me as we'd walked in the gardens at the Misty Mountain Lodge the day he'd stuck a remote-controlled plug up my ass.

Graham had told me then that he wanted to do more gardening, that it relaxed him. But he'd ended up spending so many weekends in Asheville he couldn't have had much time. That must be why the roses looked so sad. If I kept taking him away from home, would I eventually make Graham wilt the way these roses had?

CHAPTER FOURTEEN

Graham

"Avery?" He was standing by the rose garden, dressed only in a pair of sleep pants.

He turned and smiled at me. His hair was sticking up and he looked half asleep still. I wanted to devour him.

"I made coffee," he said as he walked toward where I stood on the deck.

"I saw. And I brought you a cup."

He glanced at the mugs I'd set on the bistro table. "Oh. Thank you."

"Do you mind sitting out here?"

"No, that's great."

Things were back to feeling too polite, too distant between us. I had to find a way to fix that, so I resisted the urge to touch him as he walked past me to the table. Touching would lead to kissing and that would lead to one of us pulling the other back inside and neither of us getting coffee for a long time. I needed coffee, but more importantly, Avery and I needed to talk.

Avery took a sip from his mug and looked back toward the rose garden. "You planted those roses after Felicity's wedding, didn't you?"

I nodded.

"And you haven't had time to take care of them, because you've been coming up to visit me most weekends."

I frowned, not wanting to admit that. "It's just been too hot for them."

He raised his brows, obviously not buying it.

"You're a lot more important than a few plants."

"But you wanted to do more gardening, and I'm keeping you from it. I'm keeping you from all of this." He gestured at the yard and the house.

"All you're keeping me from is a giant house where I live by myself, surrounded by things I mostly didn't even choose for myself."

"The glassware? Did you pick that out?"

I nodded. "My grandmother collected depression glass. I inherited some of her pieces and can't resist looking for more when I get a chance."

"I think your house is beautiful, but why do you live here if it's not what you want?"

I shrugged. "I like the yard and the lake. After Louise kicked me out and did her best to keep the kids away from me, I felt like I had something to prove. I needed to show that I could have anything, a huge house, a fancy car, an expanding business. I made sure whatever I bought was the best. But that was petty and stupid, and I'd rather spend my time in Asheville with you than here alone."

"You could've asked me to come to Charlotte before now, unless you didn't want me here."

Those words stole my breath. How could he think— "I came to Asheville because I love being there, because I want to give you what you need, because you had to work on Saturdays so me spending the weekend

151

there made sense. Never once did I mean to make you feel—"

"It's okay. I'm sorry. I'm just… I'm scared, Graham. This seems so much harder the more time we spend together. I just don't know what we should do."

"What if you just let Daddy make all the decisions? Would that be easier?" As soon as the words were out of my mouth, I regretted them.

Avery's eyes went wide. His mouth opened and closed, but he didn't say anything.

"I'm sorry. That was out of line. I just wanted you to know that's an option, because sometimes you've found that easier."

"I don't think that's the right choice for us, but… it's tempting, because no matter how worried I am about us finding our way, calling you Daddy still feels so right."

"It feels right to me too, boy. And all the things you think I'll miss here are things I could do in Asheville: gardening, glass collecting, discovering new restaurants to try."

"Playing the piano?"

I nodded, wishing I'd been with him when he saw the music room. I would've played for him. Hopefully I would eventually. "Pianos can be moved. Before I met you, I'd forgotten how much I'd loved all those things. You helped me remember there's so much more for me than work and quick hookups. I hadn't played the piano in years. I don't even know what possessed me to buy one for this house, but since I met you, I've started playing again."

"Really?"

"Yes, Avery." I squeezed his hand.

"But what about your friends? I could tell last night how close you are. I don't want to take you away from them."

I sighed. "Leo will be spending lots of time in Asheville, and I'm sure Max and Foster will visit too once he's running Thrust. I care about all of them, but with all our work schedules, we don't see each other often. I can drive to Charlotte to spend a few days with them if I want to, and I'd like to bring you back and let you get to know them better."

"It was hard last night; you all have this history, and…" He looked away, seeming unsure how to finish.

"I'm sorry. I didn't mean for you to feel left out."

"You didn't do anything wrong, and neither did they. I just feel like you have this whole life here, and it's so different from what you have with me."

"Different, yes, but you're what I want, what I've been longing for. I can hold on to my friendships from a distance, but I can't fully share my life with you like I want to if we're apart. To do that, we need to live in the same town, or even together."

He gave me a disbelieving look. "I just told you I'm not sure how we can make this work, and you're asking me to move in with you?"

I took a slow breath, knowing I had to tread carefully. "I'm telling you I'm open to that. I'd love for us to live together, because I want to share everything with you, all the things I want to do, the places I want to go. I want to take you to Tuscany and Scotland, and all the places you've dreamed of, but you have to let me. You have to be comfortable with me giving you all that I want to give."

"I want to do all those things, but it feels wrong to take from you."

"Does it feel wrong to take from me when it's pleasure?"

He shook his head. "That's different from things that cost money."

"It's just as valuable, more so really, because the feeling you give me when you open yourself for me isn't something I can work for, or study for, it's a gift."

Tears shone in his eyes. "Oh, Daddy. I… I'm sorry, maybe I should call you Graham right now."

I laid a hand on his arm. "Let's not worry about those boundaries. Just use whatever name feels natural."

"Surrendering to you feels natural."

"I know, boy. No matter how you feel about anything else, I know that, and I know that being comfortable with me spending money on you isn't the same as giving me control in other ways."

"Neither is agreeing for you to move. I know you don't need my permission, but—"

I took both his hands in mine. "I want everything we do to be consensual, including me moving."

He looked at our joined hands and sighed. "I need some time to think."

"Then take it."

"But—"

"If you want to, you can still stay the weekend, or you can go on back to Asheville and take the time you need." I wasn't sure how I got those words past the lump in my throat.

"Daddy, I don't want to leave you." His voice sounded as choked as mine.

"I'm not breaking up with you or even telling you to leave. You can stay here as long as you want. I'm just promising to give you as much time as you need to figure things out. That's the best way for me to care for you right now. No matter how much I want to hold you tight and not let go, that's not the kind of daddy you need now. You need your freedom."

He slid out of his chair and knelt by me, laying his head on my thigh. "You're too good to me."

"No, I'm not. I'm just trying to give you what you need."

"I know you must think I'm crazy. You're offering me everything and—"

I used a finger under his chin to make him look at me. "No, Avery. I'm asking a lot and probably pushing way too hard."

"You know what you want and I… I thought I did. Maybe I do, but…"

"It's okay. Take time to think about what you can handle, and please know this isn't an ultimatum. I'm not saying that if you aren't ready for me to move to Asheville, we have to end this."

He looked even paler than he had a few moments before. "I don't want to end it."

"I know, baby. It's going to be okay."

Tears rolled down his cheeks and wet the leg of my jeans. I carded my fingers through his hair as he cried.

A few moments later, he sat up and wiped his eyes. "Thank you for understanding, Daddy."

"You don't need to thank me for giving you room to breathe. Any decent person would do that."

"You're so much more than decent."

I stroked his cheek. "You're a good boy. Whatever you decide won't change that."

I rose and pulled Avery up and into my arms. "Let me make you breakfast. Then, if you're ready, you can go home and call Felicity or Sean or someone you trust and talk this out."

"You don't mind me talking about all this with Felicity?"

"She's your best friend. I won't take that from you just because I might blush when I see her again."

He smiled for the first time since our conversation had begun. "I'm not going to give her any details. I'm not that perverted."

"Are you sure?"

His eyes widened, but then he grinned. "Daddy! I'm shocked."

"I'd need to do more than that to shock you."

"Why don't you see if you can come up with something?" His smile faded. "Um… I mean… Whenever… If we…"

What if he went back to Asheville and decided he wanted to end things? I wouldn't be with him like this again. I looked away for a moment and cleared my throat, wishing I didn't have to face this reality. "Do you want pancakes with your bacon, or eggs and toast? The bacon is not negotiable."

"Oh, really." He pressed his lips together, like he was trying to hold in a laugh.

"Yes, really." At least I could still entertain him. "Pancakes, please."

"Coming right up." I prayed I could get through breakfast without breaking down and begging him to stay.

CHAPTER FIFTEEN

AVERY

Almost two weeks had passed since I'd seen Graham. I'd cried most of the drive back to Asheville and then slept for fourteen hours. In the days since, I'd talked to Felicity, Sean, a few other stylists at my salon, and even, strangely enough, Carter and his sister Mandy. All of them essentially told me to get my head out of my ass and accept Graham's money as well as his offer to move.

"It doesn't make you a kept man; you're still working. Would the bank be your sugar daddy if you got a loan for your business? I think not," Felicity had said.

Carter's statement on the situation: "Look, I might not like to talk about you and Dad, but you're good together, really good, and I don't want either of you to lose that. Just let him take care of you; he's good at it."

And Mandy had said, "My dad can be a pushy bastard sometimes, but he totally means well, and I think he's crazy about you. You've wanted your own company for like ever. So put him out of his misery, let him help you, and go look at houses with him."

I hadn't slept well since I'd left Charlotte. And now here I was on Thursday night, lying in bed, staring at the ceiling with no idea how late it had gotten or how

I'd get enough sleep to get through work the next day. Then my phone rang. It was Wren. Was he calling to tell me off too?

I answered with "Yes, I know I'm an idiot."

"Is my dad there?" He sounded shaken up.

"No, we're not… We're taking some time apart. I thought you knew that."

"Yeah, Mandy told me, but I figured you were back together by now. You seem to fit so well."

Wow, even Wren saw that, and he'd only had dinner with us once.

"Are you okay?"

"I… not exactly. I called Carter and Mandy, and they didn't answer so then I tried Dad, but he didn't answer either, so I thought maybe he was there. I…"

"What's wrong?"

"Um… I need some help."

He really didn't sound good. "Are you hurt?"

"No." His answer was quick and sharp, making me doubt him.

"Where are you?"

"I'm at Thirsty's Billiards. Can you come get me?"

"Of course, where is it?"

He gave an address, but I only vaguely recognized the street name. I thought it was somewhere north of downtown.

"And please hurry. There's this guy, and he… I don't know when he's going to come back."

"Do I need to call the police?"

"No, just come get me."

"Wren, I—"

He ended the call.

Fuck. I dressed as quickly as I could, leaving the house without even looking in the mirror. Once I was in my car, I typed the address into my GPS app and took off. The directions had me turn onto Merrimon from Chestnut Street and head north for a few blocks. When I turned onto a side street, I saw small rundown houses, interspersed with a convenience store and a tattoo shop that didn't look like it would meet any health codes. When I found Thirsty's, I could tell it would make my favorite dive bar look like the poshest restaurant in town. Fortunately, Wren was standing outside, so all I had to do was pull up at the curb and wave to him. He jumped in, and I made a U-turn and headed home.

He didn't say anything for the first few minutes of the drive. I figured the most important thing to do was to get him home. He was shivering, and he'd pulled his legs up and had his arms wrapped around them.

"Do you want me to turn the A/C down?"

"N-no. I'm fine."

He was definitely not fine.

"Wren, what happened?"

He sighed and pressed his forehead against his knees. "I was meeting a guy, but he wanted something I didn't. I'm okay. I just needed to get away."

"Wren, should I call the police? Or take you to the hospital?"

He shook his head. "No. Really. It didn't get that far."

"You have a black eye."

He laughed, but it wasn't funny at all. "So does he."

"Good. But that doesn't mean—"

"I got away before anything really happened."

159

He didn't elaborate, and I didn't push.

When we turned onto my street, he glanced around. "Where are we going?"

"My apartment."

"Can't you just take me home?"

"Sean's visiting his mom in Blowing Rock for the weekend, so there won't be anyone else there. I don't think you should be alone right now."

"I guess you're right."

"I can take you home once you're feeling more steady," I said as I pulled up at the curb in front of my building. "Unless there's a chance this guy knows where you live?"

Wren shook his head. "He doesn't even know my name."

That didn't guarantee anything, but I wanted to get Wren in the house before I asked more questions.

A little while later, Wren had taken a hot shower and was sitting on my couch, covered with a thick blanket, drinking a cup of peppermint tea. He'd said he couldn't eat anything, but he was happy to have something hot to wrap his hands around.

"I feel so stupid. I can't stop shaking."

"Wren, it's okay to be scared. You don't have to apologize for anything you're feeling."

He gave me a weak smile. "Thanks."

"Do you feel like telling me more now? You said you were meeting this guy?"

Wren sighed. "I guess I owe you an explanation."

"No, you don't, but I'd like to know so I can help you. Or would you like me to call your dad?"

He frowned. "You'd do that even though things are… not right between you?"

"Of course I would."

"Thanks. But no, I don't want him to know, and I... I can't tell him all this."

I laid my hand over his. "Then tell me."

"I met this guy through an app. He said he was... look, I know this is probably going to sound wrong, but I wasn't just looking for a regular hookup. I like... um..."

"Wren, I'm probably crossing so many lines right now, but helping you matters more. I'm into BDSM, mostly spanking, nothing too hardcore but I like to surrender to men."

"Y-you do?"

I nodded.

His eyes widened and then he grimaced. "Oh, God, that means..."

"Don't think too much about it. Just understand that I'm not going to judge you, no matter what you like."

"I like pain, okay?" His face was bright red, and he looked away as soon as he said it.

It didn't take much effort to figure out what was going on.

"This guy. He didn't care if everything was consensual?"

Wren nodded. "I tried to tell him what I liked, or what I thought I would like. I haven't really... I don't have much experience yet. But he didn't listen. I tried to fight him, but if it hadn't been for a couple of other guys who heard, he might have... I don't know how far he would've gone."

"Wren, did he rape you?" I hated even saying that word, but I had to ask.

Wren shook his head. "He slapped me and said he was going to use his knife on me. I told him no. I just wanted to start slow, just like… I don't know… not that. I got up to leave, and he hit me. I hit him back and then some guys came, and he eventually got thrown out."

I scooted closer to Wren and wrapped my arm around him. "This guy. He was a predator, not a Dom. No reasonable person would start with knife play."

Wren nodded. "I know. I've read about how to… I thought…" He dropped his head into his hands. "I'm such an idiot."

"No, you're not, but you probably shouldn't try to find what you need through an app, at least not without going to meet them for coffee or something first."

"I didn't want to tell anyone. My dad doesn't even know I'm bi."

"But you still called him."

"I was scared, and I knew he'd come for me no matter what I'd done."

"Yeah, he would." I wished I could tell Graham what Wren had said. He'd be so happy to know his son thought of him that way.

Wren studied me for a few moments. "When I called you, the first thing you said… What did you mean?"

"Well, Carter, Mandy, and Felicity have already told me off, because I don't want to let your dad support me. I assumed it was your turn."

"They yelled at you, because you don't want Dad to pay for everything?"

"Not exactly, but they think I'm wrong."

"I get why you feel like you do. I didn't want to let him pay for me to go to college."

"But you let him, didn't you?"

He shrugged. "Yeah, because I needed to go, and I didn't have another way to do it without taking out a bunch of loans. And Mandy and Carter kind of made me."

"It's different for a parent to pay for college for their kids than for your… um…"

"Boyfriend?" Wren grinned at me. It was good to see him smile.

"Yeah, boyfriend,"—that term was safer than other options—"to pay for you to start a business."

"Maybe, but he just wants to make you happy."

Before I could respond to that, Wren said, "You won't tell him about tonight, will you?"

I considered that. "I don't like keeping secrets from him."

"I'm going to tell him I'm bi, but I can't tell him about what I'm into, not even if he…" Wren grimaced. "No, I can't think about that."

I laughed. "That's probably best. I do know someone else you could talk to, though. Someone who could help you to find what you want safely. His name is Leo, and he's a friend of your dad."

"Oh yeah. Dad's mentioned him before."

"Did you know he ran a kink club?"

"What? I thought he owned a bar."

"Well, there's a bar there, but that's not all. He's thinking about buying a club here called Thrust."

Wren nodded. "I went there once, but I was too afraid to talk to anyone."

I was lucky I hadn't run into him there. Or that he hadn't seen his dad spanking me. We'd have to be way more careful going there in the future. "Leo's a Dom, and he does a lot of teaching. I'm sure he could help you find someone to introduce you to the things you want to try, someone who would go slow and be very certain he had your full consent."

"But will he tell Dad?"

"No, confidentiality is really important to him, to everyone who does this right. I think Leo's actually in Asheville tonight. I could text him. He's going to be better at helping you with this than I am. Plus you don't have to think about me and—"

"Stop!" Wren covered his ears.

"Right."

He looked up at me. "I'll let you text him under one condition."

"What is that?"

He looked mischievous now, more like himself. "Actually two."

"Tell me."

"You can't tell him my real name or who my father is."

"And?"

"You have to go see Dad. He misses you, and he just wants to take care of you."

"So you do think I'm an idiot?"

He shrugged. "Pretty much."

I narrowed my eyes at him.

"Not as big of one as me, though." He was smiling, but I could see the brittleness in his expression, so I squeezed his hand.

"Look at me. You made some unwise choices, but it's not your fault this man tried to hurt you. He did that, not you. You're a wonderful person, and there is nothing wrong with what you want. You'll find someone who can be what you need."

"Like you did with Dad?"

Oh shit, I totally had. What was I doing?

"Dad'll probably get to his condo around six tomorrow night to drop off his stuff. He's supposed to meet me, Mandy, and Carter for dinner at seven, but we won't mind if he's late."

"He's coming here?" I'd thought I'd have to go to Charlotte to see him, so I could put it off until Sunday.

Wren nodded.

Fuck. I had to do this, because Wren was absolutely right. I had found exactly what I needed with Graham. He just wanted to take care of me. I could let him do that. "I still have a key to the condo. I'll be there before six. And I won't tell Leo who you are."

"Then go ahead and contact him."

I sent him a text. *If you're where you can, call me. I need a favor.*

My phone rang a few minutes later. When I answered, the first thing Leo said was, "I hope this is a favor to get you and Graham back together. He's going crazy without you, and I'm tired of hearing him whine."

I smiled at the phone. So Leo was going to push me too. "It's not, but as it happens I'm going to see Graham tomorrow."

"I hope you're going to show him some houses you've picked out, so he can move up here and stop making me miserable."

Wow. "I haven't gotten that far yet."

"Well, hurry up. And tell me how I can help you."

"I have a friend who wants to explore submission and pain play. He had a bad encounter tonight with someone who wanted to take advantage of his needs."

"Who's the asshole, and was it at Thrust?"

"No connection to Thrust. He met this guy through an app, and we only know his user name."

"Give it to me, and I'll track the bastard down."

"I'll let my friend do that. I was hoping you'd talk to him and help him find the right person to explore with. I didn't know who else to call."

"Is your friend with you?"

"Yes."

"Are you at your apartment? I can be there in half an hour."

"I didn't mean you had to come tonight."

"He's going to need to talk, and he's lucky to have you, but I've done training in counseling. If he's comfortable with me, then I'll talk to him, and we'll set up another time to meet."

"That's awesome. Thank you."

"I've worked very hard to keep the kink community safe for people. No one should have to deal with an asshole who wants to use them instead of accepting their surrender as a gift."

"You're the best, Leo. Graham is lucky to have you as a friend." Wren's eyes went wide, and I shook my head, trying to communicate that I wasn't going to reveal who he was.

"Just promise me you really will talk to Graham tomorrow. I'm lucky to have him as a friend, and I love that you make him happy. So get over the fact that he wants to give you the world and just let him."

"Yes, sir." I gave him my address, and he told me he'd be there soon.

CHAPTER SIXTEEN

GRAHAM

I frowned as I rode up in the elevator, dreading being in the condo without Avery. As if I didn't miss him enough in Charlotte, I would think of him nonstop while I was here. This space had only ever been ours. But I wasn't going to back out on my monthly get-together with my kids. I was thankful they wanted to get together like this, and I could tell something was up with Wren. He'd called me late last night, but I'd put my phone on Do Not Disturb, trying futilely to get some sleep. When I texted him back, worried something was wrong, he told me he was fine, that he'd called my number by mistake. I wasn't sure I believed him, though. Hopefully I'd find out what was up tonight.

I dragged my suitcase down the hall and unlocked the door. When I pushed it open, I froze. Avery was there, sitting on the couch.

"I hope you don't mind that I let myself in."

"No. This place is as much yours as mine. I just wasn't expecting you."

"I know, but I've been thinking."

"You have?" My heart pounded. Was he here to end things? His expression was so neutral I couldn't tell. But he was wearing my favorite pink lipstick, shimmery gold eyeshadow, and the cropped t-shirt I'd given him. Surely he wouldn't have put all that on if he were going to tell me he'd decided not to see me anymore.

"Graham?"

I realized I'd gotten lost in thought. Had he said something else? "Yes?"

"Are you all right?"

"Do you want the real answer?"

"Of course I do." He set his iPad on the coffee table and shifted position, drawing one leg up on the couch. "Why don't you sit down?"

I sank onto the couch beside him as I said, "I haven't been all right since you left Charlotte."

"Neither have I."

"You haven't?"

"No. I can't sleep, and I think of things I want to share with you at least ten times a day, and I… I miss you."

I nodded. "I miss you too."

"Everyone says I'm crazy not to accept what you're offering."

"Everyone?"

"Felicity. All your kids. Sean. Leo."

"Leo? Did you see him while he was up here?" If he had, then that meant he'd probably gone to Thrust without me.

Avery's face went white. "I wasn't supposed to, um…"

"We were taking time apart. If you felt like you needed to be with someone else—"

"What?"

"You went to Thrust, didn't you?" I tried to be okay with it, but I was freaking out inside. We'd said we were exclusive.

169

"Graham Hillingdon, did you really think I was going to fuck someone else when we're together?"

Wow. He'd never used my full name. "These last few weeks. We haven't been exactly—"

"You're the one who told me we weren't breaking up."

"We weren't. We're not. Shit! I'm sorry. I should never have assumed that."

"Damn right you shouldn't. I would never be with someone else without talking to you, not after we agreed to be exclusive. Leo came here, but I… um… promised him I wouldn't say anything. He didn't want you to know he was trying to get me to talk to you."

"Then you… You're…" I stopped myself, not sure what was okay to say and what wasn't.

"I'm what?"

"Still my good boy?"

He smiled. "Yes, Daddy. I don't think it was very good of me to wait this long to talk to you, but—"

"You've done exactly what I told you to do."

He took a deep breath. "I guess I have."

"And I don't care what anyone else thinks you should do. I only care about what you want."

"I want you. I want you to move here. I want to explore just how far we want the Daddy/boy play to go. I want to start my own company, but I want you to be a part owner instead of just giving me money."

"Wow. That's… wow." I felt like I could finally breathe again for the first time in two weeks.

He grinned. "I even thought…"

"What? Avery, you can say anything to me."

"I thought maybe tomorrow we could go look at houses together."

"Oh my God, really? I'd love that, but I'm not sure you'll be very comfortable."

"No, I am. I'm ready to admit how much I want you to move here."

I smiled as I shook my head. "That's not what I mean. Your ass won't be comfortable."

"Oh, you have plans for me, Daddy?"

"Big plans." I made a fist with one hand.

Avery's eyes widened. "Oh, Daddy."

"I promised you I'd give you all of this, but the timing wasn't ever right. So I told myself that if you still wanted me, I'd reward you."

"Please." The word came out as a whimper.

I glanced down and saw Avery's cock pressing against his jeans. "Come here, boy."

He was in my arms in less than a second. I cupped his face and kissed him, thrusting my tongue into his mouth, claiming him. He relaxed in my arms and opened for me.

His hands gripped my hips, pulling me on top of him. I ground against him, and he wrapped one of his legs around me, trying to get more friction. Finally I had to pull back for air.

We stared at each other as we tried to catch our breaths. "Fuck, you look hot."

He grinned. "I bet I look like a mess."

His lipstick was smeared, his hair was out of place where I'd pushed my hands into it, and his pupils were huge. "You look like you need a hard fuck."

"That's not wrong, Daddy."

"Damn, it feels good to hear you call me that again."

"I'm sorry I waited so long."

171

"Don't apologize. You needed this time. I'm just thankful you decided Daddy knows exactly what you need."

He narrowed his eyes. "That might be pushing your luck."

I reached between us and slid my hand over his cock and then between his legs, pressing my fingers against him. "That's not all I'm going to push."

"Oh, Daddy. I want your whole hand in me."

"I know you do. But I have dinner plans, so that's not happening tonight."

He groaned. "I know I can't ask you to cancel on your kids."

"That's right, because you're a good boy. And if it were anyone else I'd stay here with you instead."

"It's important for your family to have time together."

"It is. And I love that you understand that." I rubbed my thumb over his plump lower lip. "Does my good boy have what he needs to stay here for a few nights?"

"No, sir."

"Go back to your apartment, pack, and then come back here. When I get home you will be in bed, wearing sleep pants. You won't touch yourself. You'll just go to sleep. If you're good, then tomorrow you'll get what you need."

"I need my ass filled, Daddy."

"I know, boy, and I'm going to love hearing the sounds you make as I open you up."

He bit his lip and whimpered.

"Just like that, only way more intense."

"Oh, fuck."

"Are you going to be good?

"Yes, Daddy."

"All right." I glanced at my watch and sighed. "I'd better get going."

"Graham?"

I let go of him and stepped back, heart pounding. Had I gone too far? "Yes?"

"I just wanted to say that this feels so right. I haven't felt this good, this settled, like everything is as it should be, since I left you in Charlotte. I love playing like this with you."

"I love this too. And I feel the same way."

He rose up on tiptoe and kissed me gently. "I'm so glad I found you."

"Me too, more than I can say."

"All right. You better go. I'll do everything you said. I promise."

"I know you will." And I'd do my best not to spend the dinner thinking only of how I wanted to be back here wrapped around him.

***

I could hear Avery moving around in the kitchen. Was he making breakfast? I should get up, make sure he ate something good for him and that he had everything he needed for work. But he'd said I didn't have to be Daddy every minute of the day, and the bed felt so good. Would he mind if I just stayed here where it was warm and it smelled like him? I rolled over on my stomach and pressed my face into Avery's pillow.

As I breathed in his scent, I worked my hips against the bed, though I wasn't really serious about getting myself off. If Avery were there, I'd order him to suck my cock, the feel of his tight lips would—No, he didn't have time to play before work, and I had plans for tonight. Plans we were going to wait for.

I groaned as I forced myself to roll over on my back. Despite my resolve, my hand slipped under the covers, and I gripped my cock. I moved my fist up and down, slowly, unable to stop.

"Graham?" Avery called. "Are you—" He stopped when he reached the doorway. He had to know what I was up to. "I brought you breakfast, but it looks like you need something else."

I let go of my cock and pushed myself up so I could lean against the headboard. "We don't have time for that now."

"Are you sure?" he purred.

"Bring me my breakfast, boy."

"Yes, Daddy." His tone was mocking, but I let it go. We were teasing, not seriously trying to role play.

"Avery, is this okay, this casual way we fall partly into our roles sometimes and—?"

Avery leaned down and kissed me softly, his tongue flicking out to lick my lips as he set a breakfast tray over my lap. "It's fine. It's perfect. I'll tell you if anything makes me uncomfortable."

"Thank you."

He moved back and sat on the edge of the bed. I looked down at the tray. There was a plate with eggs and two pieces of buttered toast, little bowls with two different types of jam, a cup of coffee, and a flower from the vase on the counter.

Avery's face was scrunched up in a way that said he was nervous about my reaction.

"I don't think anyone has ever done this for me."

"Made you breakfast?"

174

"Brought it to me all special like this."

"I wanted you to feel special, because you are. I'm not sure if the eggs are very good. I think I cooked them too long."

"Hush, boy. You got up early and cooked for me; that's enough." I glanced at the time. "You don't have long before work. Did you eat breakfast?"

"I did. I ate while I was making yours."

"Good. Go finish getting ready, and then come talk to me before you go."

"Yes, Daddy. I hope the eggs are—"

"Boy, they are perfect, because you made them for me." His cheeks were pink, and I glanced down to see his cock pressing against his jeans. I loved that praise made him hard. "Actually, come here first."

Avery moved closer. I cupped his cheek and kissed him. When I pulled back, he stared at me, wide-eyed and breathless. "I'm going to do it tonight, boy." I spread my hand wide and slid it down his chest, pressing into him with each of my fingers. "I'm going to have all this inside you."

Avery made a strangled sound and cleared his throat. "Daddy, just hearing you say that makes me dizzy."

I chuckled. "Go finish getting ready."

The eggs were fine, not as good as the ones I made, but I'd had far worse in restaurants. I spread strawberry jam on my toast and ate it as I went through my email. A few moments later, Avery came back to the bedroom.

"I'm all ready."

"Do you have plans for lunch? You're going to need your energy tonight."

"I'll get a sandwich at the shop next to the salon."

"I'm going to check and make sure you do."

He gave me a soft smile. "Yes, Daddy."

"Come here."

He did, and I pressed my hand against the fly of his jeans. "I can just imagine my slutty boy sneaking into the bathroom at work to get off, but don't you dare touch yourself today. I want you primed and ready to go off when my fist is buried in you."

He groaned. "Now I'm going to be hard all day."

I smirked at him. "Go. I'll see you tonight."

Taunting him like that had repercussions. I was half hard most of the morning as I tried to force myself to catch up on work. Then I ran some errands, picking up steaks to grill for dinner and the ingredients to make blueberry cobbler. I'd noticed how quickly Avery devoured any blueberries I bought, so I thought it would be a good treat for him. And making it would keep me busy for part of the long afternoon.

I considered jerking off, because I was going to need to go really slowly with him, but I wanted to wait. If I was too revved up to take my time, I'd have Avery suck me off when he got home.

Somehow I managed to focus enough to make pie crust. When it was chilled, I put the pie together and stuck it in the oven. Then I put a dry rub on the steaks and chopped zucchini, peppers, and onions.

I uncorked a bottle of wine and set it on the counter to breathe. I'd serve him a glass while I told him more about what we would do. Hopefully, it would relax him while also making him want me just a little bit more.

I heard his key in the door soon after I'd finished stripping down and sliding into my bathrobe. When he stepped into the main room of the condo, I was waiting on the couch for him. "Did you have a good day, boy?"

He set his bag down, but his eyes never left me. "It felt twice as long as it should have, but all my appointments went smoothly."

"That's good to hear. I have something for you."

"You do?" He looked apprehensive, but his breathlessness told me he was as turned on as he was worried. A little bit of uncertainty would only make him hornier.

I untied my robe and let it fall open. "Come over here and suck my cock, Avery."

"Um… Yes, Daddy."

"Good boy."

He knelt in front of me, and I opened my legs wider and scooted lower so my head could rest on the back of the couch.

"Put your hands behind your back and use only your mouth. No teasing, no playing around. I want you to make me come, and I want you to swallow everything I give you."

"Yes, Daddy." I could tell he wanted to ask questions. This wasn't what he'd expected, but I liked the catch in his breath and the look of wariness more than I probably should.

He leaned forward and took my cock in. I groaned as he swallowed me down. His mouth was so warm, his throat tight.

I petted his head. "Such a good boy. You can take all of Daddy's cock."

He whimpered, and the vibrations felt so good.

"That's it. Take me all the way down." I gave his head a gentle push, and he took the last of me in, pressing his face against my pubic bone.

"Stay there," I ordered, holding his head, but making sure he could push back and free himself if he needed to.

He sputtered, gagging a bit, and I let go. "So good. Such a beautiful boy." I caressed his face as he sucked in air.

"More," I demanded a moment later. "Make it good, show Daddy how much you like his cock."

I held the sides of his head, and he didn't struggle at all. He just took my whole length, bobbing his head, sucking and licking me. I was close already.

"That's it, boy. I'm going to come down your throat, and you're going to take every drop."

He nodded vigorously and relaxed even more, letting me thrust up into him with no resistance.

"So good. So fucking good," I cried out as I emptied myself into him.

He looked up at me as he swallowed, and I could tell how eager he was to please me. Before I pulled out, I scooped up the cum that had leaked from the corner of his mouth and pushed it back in. He swallowed around me, making my cock jerk a final time.

When I let my cock slide from his lips, he sagged against me, head resting on my inner thigh.

"That was amazing, Daddy. I almost came in my pants."

"But you're a good boy, so you didn't."

"No, I held back because you asked me to."

I stroked his cheeks with fingers that were still sticky with cum. "That's right, boy. You're going to wait until your ass is stretched wide, until you're sure you can't take any more inside you."

"Daddy," he whimpered, sounding so needy.

"If you feel ready to stand up, I want you to go take a shower and get ready."

"Yes, Daddy."

"I'll have some wine and a few snacks for you when you come out. Then I'm going to lay you out on the bed and work you over."

"I want this so much."

"I know you do, boy. You've wanted it since our first night together, and now you've earned it."

"Thank you, Daddy."

I ran my hand over his hair. "It's going to hurt, but I'll ease you into it, so it will be good for you."

"I trust you, Daddy. I don't mind hurting for you."

My cock responded to those words, even though it should've been thoroughly sated. "This is going to make me as happy as it will you."

"I want to give you everything, Daddy." He rose then, taking a moment to steady himself.

"Be sure you're ready, boy. I don't want you getting wobbly in the shower."

"I'm all right, Daddy. But that was really intense, the way you talked to me."

I turned him to face the hallway. Then I kissed the back of his neck and along the top of his shoulder. "The thought of fisting you is making me crazy. Was anything I said too much?"

Avery shook his head. "No, I loved it."

"Good. I put some makeup out for you to wear after your shower, and I left you a robe. Don't put on anything else."

"I'll be back soon, Daddy."

I used the guest bathroom to clean myself up. Then I tried to read the thriller I'd picked up when I was grocery shopping, knowing it would take Avery a while to prep himself for tonight. But I couldn't sit still. So instead I arranged and rearranged a platter of snacks. Had I ever been this nervous before a scene? I didn't think so, not even when I'd first learned how to Dom safely.

Finally I heard the bedroom door open, and Avery stepped out. He had the robe loosely tied. His skin looked very tan next to the white fabric, and his lips were fuck-me red. He puckered up and blew me an air kiss. "How do I look, Daddy?"

"Fucking hot, as you well know."

I handed him a glass of wine and told him to sip it slowly. Then I rubbed his feet while he drank and nibbled a few crackers and pieces of fruit. His dick tented his robe the whole time.

I could tell he was getting more and more restless as I talked quietly to him about my day and what we'd have for dinner later as if it were just any other evening.

Eventually, he broke. "Daddy, when are we—"

I raised my brows. "When I say so."

He sighed. "Yes, Daddy."

"Is my boy anxious?"

"I can wait if that's what you want."

"Come here." I patted my knee.

Avery stood.

"Take your robe off first."

He let it drop from his shoulders, then placed it on the chair. He was completely naked under it like I'd asked him to be. I let my gaze skim over his body. "You're so beautiful."

"Thank you."

He sat in my lap like I'd asked, and I rubbed his back. "I know you're eager. You've fantasized about this for a long time, and we've been teasing about it, building up to it, but you don't have to do this. I'll only be upset with my boy if he lets me hurt him when he should say no."

His eyes were huge as he looked at me, and I could feel his pulse racing where I caressed his neck. "I'm going to go slow, so slow you'll probably want to beg me for more. But for you to take what I want to give you, it's best if you're desperate and needy, willing to do anything. That will help you open up and accept it all."

"You've stretched me a lot, and I had you and the dildo in me."

"I know, baby. That's why I think you're ready. You can do this."

"Please, Daddy. I want to do it now."

I brushed a kiss against his temple. "Go position yourself on your hands and knees on the bed."

"Yes, Daddy."

He left, and I took a deep breath. I could do this. I wanted to do this, but I didn't want to hurt him or push too far and risk fucking up the trust between us. Because I was completely sure that I was head over heels in love with my boy.

CHAPTER SEVENTEEN

AVERY

I positioned myself and waited for Graham with my heart racing and sweat trickling down my face. I was scared, more than I wanted to admit, but I kept telling myself if I could take a dildo and Graham's cock, then I could do this. But was that true? I knew Graham wouldn't be angry if we stopped, but I'd wanted this for so long. I wanted to know how it would feel for him to stretch me that much, and I wanted to please him. He took such good care of me. He was all I'd been longing for, and I loved him. I might not be ready to say it out loud, but it was true.

Graham stepped into the room. He was naked now too, and despite my nerves, my cock rose at the sight of his gorgeous body. His broad chest, dusted with dark hair and glints of silver. His thick cock, which jutted out, showing me he was just as into this as I was. His muscular thighs that could easily pin me in place. I wanted to worship him, but I stayed where I was.

He leaned over to kiss the back of my neck, then licked a line down my back. I hoped he would continue along my crack, but he didn't. He just squeezed my ass cheeks, pulling them apart. "I like how easily you offer your ass to me, boy."

I arched my back more deeply. "It's all yours, Daddy."

"Good boy. Now spread your legs."

I did as he said, opening wide. "It's time to get you good and wet." He bent down and swiped his tongue over my crack.

"Please."

"Mmm. I love when you beg."

"Daddy, please, put your tongue in me."

"Not yet." He teased me, circling my hole, flicking his tongue over it. I was squirming under him when he finally pushed inside me, tongue-fucking me until I was sure I was going to come.

"Daddy. I can't. Please. It's too much." A few seconds later, he sat back, and though I'd begged him to stop, I nearly cried at the loss of sensation.

He squeezed the base of my cock tightly. "You are not to come until I say so."

"I'll be good, Daddy."

"I know you will. Now that I've loosened you up some, I'm going to start stretching you."

"Yes, please, Daddy."

He greased up his fingers and pushed two into me. "Mmm, you're very tight, boy. We've got to do something about that." He worked his fingers in and out, far too slowly.

I glanced over my shoulder. "More, please!"

He slapped my ass, making me jump. "I told you we were going slow."

I shook my head, not wanting slow. "I can take a lot more."

"You remember the first night we were together? I had you just like this, and I made you wait."

"And I loved it." Sometimes I was sure he was a sorcerer to pull confessions like that from me.

"You did. So just like then, you'll take what I give you when I give it to you."

I laid my head back down on my arms. "Yes, Daddy."

"Now relax and open up for me." At least he fucked me faster now, curling his fingers against my prostate. I pushed back trying to take more, and finally, he added a third finger. The stretch felt so good, and I was more convinced than ever that I could do this.

"You're doing great, boy. Are you ready for more?"

"Yes, Daddy, please. I want this."

"I know you do." He reached under me and pinched one of my nipples. I yelped in surprise. Then he pinched it again harder, making it sting. I bit my lip, holding in a shout.

He smacked my ass again. "Your cries, your agony, they are mine. Do not hold them back."

"Yours. It's all yours." He twisted my nipple again and then pushed all four fingers into me. "Oh, fuck!"

"Talk to me, boy."

"It hurts. But… I want more. It's like too much and not enough at the same time."

He pulled all the way out and coated his hand with extra-thick lube. Then as he pushed back in, he pinched the tip of my cock and I cried out. "Daddy!"

He eased deeper as I tried to remember how to breathe. "How are you doing now?"

I shook my head. "Too much, too full. Like you're going to split me open."

"Do you want me to stop?"

"No. Please don't. I want this. I want to hurt, because I… God, I don't know."

"Shhh," he soothed, caressing my ass. "I'm here to give you what you need. It doesn't matter why you need it. I love doing this. I love seeing your ass stretched around my fingers. I love that you trust me, that you want to give yourself to me like this."

"More?" he asked after rubbing my back for a few moments.

I still couldn't breathe right. "N-not yet."

"That's okay, we're going to take our time." I watched through my spread legs as he dipped his free hand into the tub of thick lube and then rubbed it around the stretched edge of my hole. He eased his hand out and coated his fingers. "I'm going to push back in. I want you to exhale and push out, okay?"

"Yes, Daddy." He pushed in a little harder this time. "Fuck, that hurts."

"I know it does, but my thumb is in there now, boy."

Wow. Oh wow. "It is?"

"Yes, baby, we're so close."

"I... Fuck. I had no idea it would be like this. Like I really don't think this is possible, but I trust you."

He pulled his hand from me. "Turn over and look at me, boy."

I eased myself onto my side and then rolled to my back. My face felt hot, and I had to force myself to meet his gaze.

"You remember that you don't have to do this, right?" he asked.

I had to swallow and lick my lips before I could answer. "I want this. It's amazing to give myself like this, to let you do this, even though I don't think I can take it."

185

He laid a hand on my chest. "Your heart is beating so fast, boy."

I nodded. "I know."

"How do you feel?"

"My ass is on fire, and I don't even know if it hurts or feels good. But the one thing I do know is that I want more."

"Then that's what I'll give you." He pushed back in, and I got fuller and fuller and then I couldn't breathe. "No. Oh God. It's too much."

He froze. "Boy?"

I tried to find the right words. "I… I don't really mean… That's not my safeword."

He smiled. "I know, baby. I'm just checking, because you're so tense, and that's going to make it hurt more."

"I'm sorry. I… I'll try to relax. Just don't give up on me." Tears welled in my eyes, and I turned away from him.

"I will never give up on you, boy, but I also won't damage you. I'll go as slow as I have to, even if we don't get all the way today."

"We don't need to stop. Really. I just need…"

He drizzled some of our regular lube on my dick and wrapped his fingers around me. "Let's see if this helps you relax."

He used slow, firm strokes and soon, I forgot to be scared, I forgot how much all those fingers in my ass hurt. All I could think about was how much I wanted to come.

"I'm going to give you a little more, boy, okay?"

"Please!"

He pushed deeper. "Holy fuck!"

"Easy, boy." He squeezed my cock, distracting me.

"It feels like you're putting a barrel in me, not your hand."

Graham laughed. "I promise I'm not."

"O-okay."

"Just breathe. You're so close to taking it all."

He pulled out some and added even more lube. As he pushed back in, he twisted his wrist and flexed his fingers.

"Fuck! Oh, fuck!" I kept repeating my words and muttering other nonsense. By that point I was nearly out of my mind with need and want, pain and pleasure.

"Take some deep breaths, boy."

I tried to. He let go of my cock and toyed with my nipples some more. When I was able to take in enough air, I said, "I'm ready, Daddy."

He gave me just a little more, and I tried to keep breathing.

"It's so tight in there, boy. It feels like you're squeezing my hand in two."

"Yeah?"

He nodded. "And it's going to get tighter."

I swallowed hard. "I know."

"It's time to get past the widest part. I'll go slow, but I'll keep moving until I'm all the way in."

"Yes, Daddy. Please do it."

After adding more lube, he pushed in farther and farther. I was absolutely sure he was stretching me too far. I wasn't going to be able to do this. I was literally going to come apart.

"I'm in, Avery. I'm all the way in!"

"Oh my God. Oh my fucking God. We did it."

"*You* did it. You've got my whole hand inside you."

He moved then, just a little, and his fingers pushed against my prostate. The sensation was such a mix of pain and pleasure, my body didn't know whether to move into it or try to get away.

"Daddy?"

"Yes, boy."

"Do that again, please." He did, and I whined, tossing my head back and forth.

"Talk to me, boy."

"I… I want you to move, but I'm scared."

"Give yourself a little bit to adjust, and then I'll move. I promise. I'll work you until you come."

My cock had softened when he pushed in all the way, but now it was fully hard again and more than ready for Graham to do just that.

"Lift up on your elbows. I want you to see."

I did, and he picked up a hand mirror. I hadn't even realized he'd set one on the bed. He held it so I could see his hand buried in me to the wrist. "Holy fuck. Your hand. Your whole fucking hand."

"That's right, boy. You've made your daddy very proud."

"Thank you, Daddy. Thank you for giving this to me."

"You're welcome, boy. Now lie back, and I'm going to fuck you with my fist."

"Please."

He pulled out a little and poured even more lube on his hand. We were both a slippery mess, but that just added to the dirty, so-wrong-but-so-good feeling. "Hold out your hand."

I did, and he slathered it with the lube. "Jerk yourself off. I want to see you drain yourself dry while I slide my hand in and out of you."

"Oh, Daddy!"

He pushed back in all the way. It stung like hell, but my cock didn't care. I was so full, so fucking full. Graham pressed against my sweet spot, and I tightened my grip on my cock.

"That's it, boy, work that dick."

My hand moved faster and faster. Graham was sliding in and out, fucking me with his fist. "I can't believe this is real."

"It's real. I own you now. No one else has ever given you this, stretched your ass this much, filled you like you need to be filled."

"No, Daddy. No one else."

"And no one will."

"No one." I worked my cock so fast. I was right there. Graham pushed in hard, and I cried out as my climax slammed into me. "I love you, Daddy."

My ass squeezed Graham's hand as the most exquisite pleasure I'd ever felt racked my body. Cum shot over my chest, even hitting my chin.

"Look at me," Graham demanded when the tremors ceased and I floated in a world of pleasure. I had a fleeting thought that I should be embarrassed by what I'd said, but right then I didn't care. I loved him, and I wanted him to know it. I opened my eyes, though they felt so heavy.

"You're incredible, boy. I'm so proud of you."

"Daddy. I do love you."

"I know. I love you too, so much."

"I want you to come on me, Daddy."

He frowned. "It's going to hurt when I pull out, and I need to make sure you're okay."

"Daddy, please!" I was almost in tears and not sure why.

"Okay, baby. Breathe and push while I take my hand out."

I cried out when my ass stretched over the widest part of his hand. When he was all the way out, I lay there panting, feeling out of time and space and needing something to ground me.

"Are you sure you want this, boy?"

"Please. I need you, Daddy. Need you to come on me."

He rose on his knees between my legs and jerked himself so fast I'd swear his hand was a blur. "So hot, seeing you like that, impaled on me, ass stretched over my knuckles and squeezing my wrist. You're so good, so trusting. Need you, boy." He cried out as a stream of cum landed on my stomach.

"I'm yours, Daddy. I just want to be yours."

He leaned down so he could kiss me, a sweet gentle kiss that felt like he was saying "I love you" all over again.

CHAPTER EIGHTEEN

GRAHAM

I washed Avery gently and made sure his ass was okay. I'd been slow and careful as I'd opened him up, but I needed to know I hadn't hurt him. Now he was dressed in shorts and a t-shirt, lying on his side on the balcony sofa as I grilled our dinner. He'd clearly loved what we'd done, but something serious was on his mind, and I wanted it out in the open before we ate.

"Avery?"

He looked up and smiled. "Yeah?"

"What's bothering you? Did it hurt more than you expected?"

He frowned. "Yeah. Maybe. I don't know. It was so good, though. Totally worth it."

That made me smile. "I'm glad I could give you that. But you're... I don't know... off somehow."

"I'm just thinking." He fiddled with the edge of his shirt. "And I'm tired and..."

"Boy, tell me what's wrong."

He glanced up at me. "Are you going to make me?"

I took the zucchini off the grill, but I didn't put the steaks on. Instead, I walked over and knelt in front of him. "I'm not going to make you, Avery. I'm never going to make you do anything. I ask or tell you what I want, and you decide to give it to me."

He licked his lips and swallowed. Then he laid his hand on top of mine. "I know that, Daddy. I'm sorry."

"It's okay, boy." I kissed his temple. "Please talk to me."

"When you said… um… that you loved me, was that real or part of the… you know… role play?"

"Avery, I would never say something like that as part of a game. I love you. I think I've loved you since our first night together. But I know for sure I do now."

"So it's real?"

I nodded. "It's very, very real."

His face lit up then. "It's real for me too. I just wanted to be sure."

"The only things I say as a game are about tormenting you or punishing you. Everything I've said about loving and caring for you is real."

He reached for me, and I wrapped my arms around him, holding him tight. "I love you so much. I should've told you sooner."

"No, it's okay. I knew. I just… I wasn't ready to talk about it."

"And now?"

He sniffled and wiped his eyes. "Now, I'm ready."

"And you're ready for me to move here."

He nodded. "So ready. There's even… well, there's a house I want to show you that I've loved forever. It's for sale now, and…"

I cupped the side of his face. "Does that mean you'd consider living there with me?"

"I… yeah."

Oh wow. I hadn't expected him to agree to move in with me so quickly. It was everything I wanted, no matter how crazy it seemed. "Let's go see it after dinner."

He frowned. "I'm not sure I can sit in the car."

"I'll find a way to make you comfortable, baby. Because if this house means that much to you, I want to see it before anyone else snaps it up."

I insisted on feeding Avery while he lay on his side. Watching him take bites of steak as I offered them on my fork, seeing how easily he accepted me taking care of him, made my chest ache. I loved this man so much. I would do anything for him. It was going to be an adjustment for us to be together, but I believed we could handle a relationship that was more grounded in reality.

When we pulled up in front of a blue American foursquare-style home with a wrap-around porch, I knew it was the one.

"What do you think?" Avery asked, sinking his teeth into his bottom lip as he waited for my answer.

"I think I want to put up a porch swing and spend every summer evening cuddling my boy in it."

"Oh my God, really? You like it?"

"I do." I pulled out my phone and dialed the number of the real estate agent on the sign in the front yard. Despite the late hour, a woman with a cheerful voice and strong North Carolina accent answered.

"I'm interested in your listing at 158 Channing Street. I'm only in town for a few days, and I'd really like to tour it tonight."

"Oh. Yes, sir. How soon can you be there?" she asked.

"I'm actually sitting in front of it now."

193

"Well, then. If you can give me about fifteen minutes, I'll be right there to show it to you."

"That sounds perfect. Thank you."

Avery was staring at me. "We're going to go inside? Tonight."

"We are, and unless there are major structural problems, we're going to put in an offer."

"But you haven't seen any other houses."

"You want this one."

"But that—"

I laid a finger over his lips. "I love this house, Avery. I know it's right the same way I knew we were right for each other."

"You do?"

"Yes." I cupped his face. "What does your instinct tell you?"

"That I want to be on that porch swing with you."

"Then just like you did when you found me in the garden the night of Carter's wedding, forget about rules and what you should or shouldn't do, and follow your heart."

He smiled and I could see the love in his expression. "My heart told me you were the one I needed."

"Was it right?"

"So very right."

I kissed him then, a slow, soft reminder of the love between us. "I want to live in this house with you, Avery. I want to take care of you. I want to be the daddy you need and the man you want to share your life with."

"You're already all of that."

Those words warmed me all the way to my toes. "Then let's see about buying a house."
"Yes, Daddy."

Dear Reader,

Thank you for purchasing *After the Weekend*. I hope you enjoyed it. If you haven't read, *Father of the Groom (Love and Care Book 1)*, it tells the beginning of Graham and Avery's story. If you like age gap romance you may also enjoy the *Thorne and Dash* series which starts with *Professional Distance* as well as *A Chance at Love* which is a stand-alone title. I offer a free book to anyone who joins my mailing list. To learn more go to silviaviolet.com/newsletter.

Please consider leaving a review where you purchased this ebook or on Goodreads. Reviews and word-of-mouth recommendations are vital to independent authors.

I love hearing from readers. You can chat with me on Facebook in Silvia's Salon, and you can email me at silviaviolet@gmail.com. To read excerpts from all of my titles, visit my website: http://silviaviolet.com/books.

Silvia Violet

Author Bio

Silvia Violet writes fun, sexy stories that will leave you smiling and satisfied. She has a thing for characters who are in need of comfort and enjoys helping them surrender to love even when they doubt it exists. Silvia's stories include sizzling contemporaries, paranormals, and historicals. When she needs a break from listening to the voices in her head, she spends time baking, taking long walks, curling up with her favorite books, and spending time with her family.

Website: silviaviolet.com

Facebook: facebook.com/silvia.violet

Facebook Group: Silvia's Salon

Twitter: @Silvia_Violet

Instagram: instagram.com/silvia.violet

Pinterest: pinterest.com/silviaviolet

Titles by Silvia Violet

Lace-Covered Compromise
A Chance at Love
Coming Clean
If Wishes Were Horses
Revolutionary Temptation
Of Hope and Anguish
Three Under the Christmas Tree
Needing A Little Christmas

Love and Care
Father of the Groom
After the Weekend

Fitting In
Fitting In
Sorting Out
Burning Up
Going Deep
Getting Hitched

Thorne and Dash
Professional Distance
Personal Entanglement
Perfect Alignment
Well-Tailored (A Thorne and Dash Companion Story)

Ames Bridge
Down on the Farm
The Past Comes Home
Tied to Home

After the Weekend

Unexpected
Unexpected Rescue
Unexpected Trust
Unexpected Engagement

Law and Supernatural Order
Sex on the Hoof
Paws on Me
Dinner at Foxy's
Hoofing' It To The Altar

Wild R Farm
Finding Release
Arresting Love
Embracing Need
Taming Tristan
Willing Hands
Shifting Hearts
Wild R Christmas

36241830R00120

Printed in Poland
by Amazon Fulfillment
Poland Sp. z o.o., Wrocław